GLORIA MONTERO

Billy Higgins Rides the Freights

Illustrated by Olena Kassian

James Lorimer & Company, Publishers
Toronto 1982

Canadian Cataloguing in Publication Data

Montero, Gloria, 1933-
  Billy Higgins rides the freights

ISBN 0-88862-578-2 (bound). — ISBN 0-88862-579-0 (pbk.)

1. Depression — 1929 — Canada — Juvenile fiction.
I. Title.

PS8576.058B55   jC813'.54   C82-094173-5
PZ7.M65Bi

0-88862-578-2 cloth
0-88862-579-0 paper

Design: Michael Solomon

Teacher's guide available from the publisher.
Write to the address below.

The
Adventure in Canada
Series

James Lorimer & Company, Publishers
Egerton Ryerson Memorial Building
35 Britain Street
Toronto, M5A 1R7, Ontario

Printed and bound in Canada

For Red Walsh
and other Canadian heroes
of the Depression

Contents

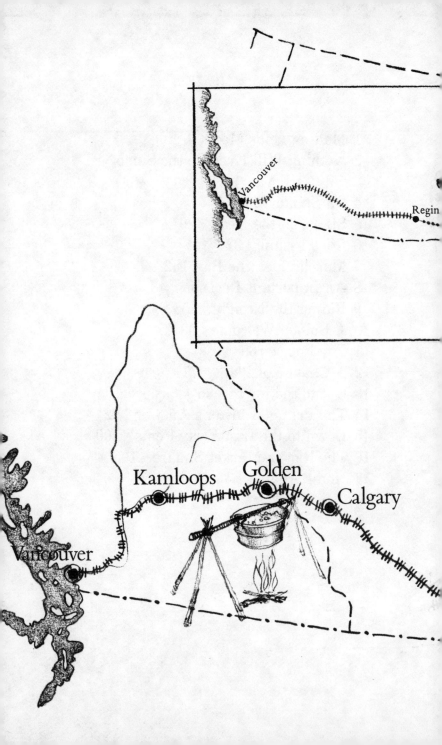

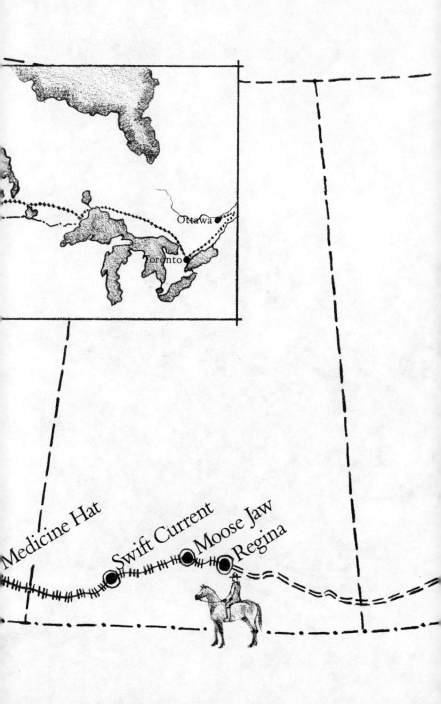

1

Making Ends Meet

IF you ever hear of someone losing his job, you can be sure there's a long story there somewhere. It happened to Billy Higgins's dad, and the life of the whole family was turned upside down.

First of all I should explain a bit about the Higgins family. There were four of them: Sam, his wife, Mary, twelve-year-old Billy, and Helen, just turned ten. They lived on Cameroon Street in Vancouver in a little wooden house that Sam was forever fixing up.

Sam Higgins was a tool and die maker. You need a lot of skill for that kind of work. You've got to know all about metals and how to cut and shape them — and also how the big cutting machines and presses work. Billy went twice with his father to the machine shop and saw some of those machines cutting steel the way a pair of scissors cuts paper. They were that powerful. Because Sam was very good at his work, he'd held the same job for seventeen years at Robertson's Machine Shop out in New Westminster.

Mary, Sam's wife, had long red hair, the greenest eyes you've ever seen, and a temper that could flash without warning. She grew vegetables around the side of the house, and it was too bad for the neighbourhood cats and dogs that came and scratched among her carrots and beans!

Billy was a tall, skinny boy, big for his age. He was already taller than his dad, and he had his mother's green eyes and red hair. In addition, he had the worst case of freckles imaginable. They covered every square inch of his face and his arms. They were so big and brown that you could hardly see the pale white skin underneath.

Billy hated his freckles. He thought they were ugly, and he envied the smooth brown skin of his friend Alfie Baker. Alfie could stay out in the sun for hours and hours and he just got more tanned. Billy felt that Alfie's freckleless dark skin must be one of the nicest things about being an Indian.

Helen had neither freckles, red hair nor green eyes. She was short and dark haired like her father. As far as Billy was concerned, there was only one thing that made living with Helen difficult. She always wanted to tag along after him. They were good friends, but this was sometimes a nuisance. Either she'd want to go fishing with him and Alfie up the creek behind where Alfie's uncle lived, or else she'd nag Billy to let her play baseball with the boys on the old diamond back of the garbage dump. Since some of Billy's friends didn't really want a girl tagging along, Billy would yell at Helen to go play with her own friends.

The Higginses had an old, green Chevy sedan that Sam had bought from Scobie, the foreman at the machine shop. Scobie bought himself a shiny, new Ford, one of those sporty models with a rumble seat in the back. He took Billy and Helen for a ride in it one day. They felt like movie stars, sitting up there with the wind racing through their hair and everyone staring at them as they went by.

Even without a rumble seat the old, green Chev was worth having. The Higginses used it for their holidays up the coast. Sometimes, Sam and Billy took the Chev over to Vancouver Island on the ferry. They'd spend the whole weekend there, catching salmon on the inlet up near Port Alberni.

The Higgins family had a lot of fun together. Sam was a great crossword puzzle man. On Saturday nights while the others were sitting around listening to the radio and killing themselves laughing over the antics of Fibber McGee and Molly, Sam would be looking for words. "What would a nation of Indians be that has five letters and ends in an x?" or "What has eight letters, starts with a c, ends with an l, and wears either red feathers or a hat?" he'd call out. The others would help him out if they could, unless their radio program was too exciting. Those were warm and happy times.

One morning everything changed for the Higgins family. Sam went in to work and learned that Robertson's was going out of business. Mr. Robertson himself came to speak to the employees. He was a worried-looking little man in a pale grey suit. He explained that no one was ordering the parts for washing machines that the shop made. Hardly anyone seemed to be buying washing machines anymore. He had no choice but to close down.

When Sam came home and told his family that he'd lost his job, Mary was shocked and worried about how they would live, but she didn't cry or go on about it. She just told Sam, "We'll have to make ends meet as best we can."

And they did — though making ends meet became harder and harder as time went on. Sam got what work he could. For a while he worked in a fish cannery, but when the season ended, he was laid off again. After that he delivered firewood around the city in a horse-drawn wagon. Then before Christmas he got a job sorting mail at the post office. That only lasted for a few weeks.

They had to sell the old, green Chev because they couldn't afford to pay for gas or even to renew the licence. "It'll be better to have the money in the bank than sitting out in the garage," Sam joked. But the money from the sale of the car didn't last long.

About the same time they sold the car, their telephone was cut off. Even those few extra dollars every month were more than the family budget could bear.

Billy wore old hand-me-downs of his father's, mainly shirts and sweaters because his father's pants were too short for him. He inherited an old pair of Sam's black shoes. They fitted him all right, but his mother had to cut new cardboard soles to cover the holes in the leather.

"I'm tired of being poor," Billy complained one day as his mother tried to let down the cuffs on some pants he'd outgrown. "Why can't Dad make some real money?"

"It's not your dad's fault," snapped his mother, a needle held between her lips. "We're in the Depression. Nearly everyone's out of work. Now hold still."

"Can't someone do something about it?" Billy asked. "It's not fair that we should all have to sit around and suffer."

"Well, there's nothing we can do. Now stop being so restless, or I'll poke you with this needle. Honestly, you're just like all my brothers, headstrong and unable to sit still for a minute. It'll get you into trouble some day."

After the post office job Sam couldn't get any work at all. Every day there seemed to be more men like himself walking the streets looking for a job. Most of them were prepared to do anything, but there wasn't anything to do.

Finally, like most of the others, Sam had to ask the city for help, or "relief" as everyone called it. Once a week he'd take a sack to the old church building on the Cambie Street grounds and join the gunnysack parade. He'd get potatoes, beef, pork, butter, sugar, tea, coffee, rolled oats, flour, baking powder and salt.

When Sam arrived home with his sack, it would seem like an enormous load of groceries. But no matter how carefully Mary planned their meals, there was never much food left after three or four days. Billy always knew it was the end of the week by the hunger pains in his stomach when he went to bed.

Those days were grim indeed. Billy even lost his best friend. Alfie Baker had been sent back to Vancouver Island to his grandmother on the reserve.

Alfie's parents were both dead. From the time he was four years old, Alfie had lived with his uncle Frank down near the creek not far from Billy's own house. From the day they'd both started school, Alfie had been Billy's best friend. They spent a lot of time together, fishing, playing ball, and just hanging around.

Once, Billy had even gone with Alfie for two whole weeks to his grandmother's house on the Island. It had been wonderful. Right next door to Alfie's grandmother lived a young man they all called Tassie. He was trying to make a totem pole. Tassie told the boys that he wanted to make a pole just like his great-grandfather had made. He showed them a picture of a tall painted log carved into mask-like faces, with a huge eagle, his wings outspread, sitting right at the top.

Every day from morning till night Tassie worked on that pole. Billy and Alfie used to sit around and watch him concentrate over the stern, strange faces he was cutting in the wood.

Tassie showed the boys how to carve simple figures with a sharp knife. When Billy came home, he brought a seagull he'd made himself from an old scrap of pine. He painted it grey and white, with yellow on the legs and the beak. His mother still had it on top of the sideboard beside the radio.

One day, when Billy and his mother were worrying about money, Billy picked the bird up. "Maybe I could carve a lot of these and sell them to tourists," he said to his mother. "That would help a little bit."

"Not many tourists around these days, Billy," said his mother with a smile. "Nobody has the money to travel, much less buy wood carvings."

"Come on, you treat me just like a kid."

"I don't mean to. It's a real nice bird."

"Well, it was only my first try."

Billy had made the legs a bit too long for the body, and Alfie had always kidded him about it. He'd said it looked more like a stork than a seagull. Now Alfie was gone. Who knew when they'd be able to share more good times together?

The Higginses had to learn to do without a lot of things. What did help to make it bearable was the fact that almost every other family they knew shared the same sort of difficulties.

Even though times were hard, there still were some special days to look forward to. Like Billy's thirteenth birthday. The date was circled in red on the calendar that hung near the stove in the little house on Cameroon Street: February 27, 1935.

2

Nothing Will Ever Be the Same

RIGHT from the minute he opened his eyes, Billy knew this would be a special day. He had the feeling in his stomach that you get before something really important happens to you. What Billy didn't know, of course, was that after this day nothing in his life would ever be quite the same again.

It was a wonderful birthday. His father gave him a new fly that was supposed to be a sure-fire way to catch trout, and his mother had knitted him a navy blue sweater with a scarf to match. But it was Helen's gift that surprised Billy most of all.

When she handed him the flat, awkward parcel wrapped in newspaper, he had no idea what the present was going to be. She had coloured the newspaper with crayons to make it look pretty, like expensive wrapping paper. Even after shaking and squeezing it, Billy couldn't guess what was inside.

Then he unwrapped it and discovered the sling-shot. It was a beauty. And the amazing thing was that Helen had made it herself. She had found a forked piece of driftwood along the beach. It was smooth to hold and had a lovely, shiny grey colour. From an old inner tube she had cut two narrow strips of rubber. At the end of each strip she'd attached a square of soft leather. Billy recognized the leather as the tongue from the old brown shoes he had outgrown. Helen had cut two holes in the leather and carefully tied the rubber strips in neat knots through each hole. On the handle she had carved his initials: B.H.

"I swear, Helen, you're just asking for trouble, giving your brother a thing like that," said his mother, shaking her head. "He's just itching to get into trouble, and this won't help a bit."

"Don't be silly, Mum," Billy said with a laugh. "I'm not going to use it on people."

"What's it for, then?"

"Well, I don't know. Target practice."

"I hope so."

The slingshot worked like a charm. When he put a small round stone in it, Billy was able to shoot it all the way over to the corrugated-iron shed where fat old Harry Tomlin kept his chickens. The stone made a terrible bang when it hit the shed. Old Tomlin came out shaking his fist at Billy, swearing at him and threatening to report him to the police.

Billy and Helen laughed a lot over this. Old Tomlin was always raving mad about something. And when he got mad, his fat face and belly would shake with rage. People joked that he couldn't have gotten that fat on the scrawny chickens he kept out in the shed. "It's more likely to be from the bottles of booze he brings home in those paper bags," Mary Higgins claimed. "Still, I don't want any trouble with the police, Bill, and I mean it. Can't you stay home and sit still once in a while?"

That night, for Billy's special birthday dinner, a square cake stood in the middle of the dining room table. It was decorated with a big red BILLY 13. For weeks Mary had been saving up flour and butter from the gunnysack food to make the birthday cake. The red letters were spelled out in coloured sugar. Helen told Billy the sugar was coloured with the juice of a squashed-up bug. Billy, sure she was teasing him, started to chase her around the room, but his mother told him it was true. The cochineal was a tropical insect that came from Mexico and Central America. It was so tiny that you needed thousands of the little bugs to have enough to make one small jar of red food colouring. Billy made such a face at the thought that his mother laughed and assured him the dye was quite safe to eat.

It made Billy feel good to see his name spelled out with the number thirteen right there beside it. Even if the sugar was coloured red with little tropical bugs, that cake was quite a sight. Before eating it, they had a delicious Irish stew with bits of meat and lots of potatoes.

For the party everyone wore paper crowns of different colours. Mary's crown was blue, Helen's was yellow, Sam wore a green crown, and Billy's crown was a brilliant red — to match the letters on his cake.

When they sang "Happy Birthday," Mary conducted the rest of the family in the singing. She looked funny waving her arms as if she had the whole school choir in front of her instead of just Sam and Helen, but to Billy she sure made them sound good.

There was a lot of laughter at the table. They all kept asking if anyone would care for a drop more champagne. That was a family joke. Mary had made special labels, with FRENCH CHAMPAGNE written in big green letters, to cover the ordinary ginger ale labels on the bottles. "Anyway, it's got the same bubbles," Helen said quite seriously. She really liked ginger ale.

After dinner, while Helen and Mary cleared away the dishes, Sam told Billy he wanted to talk to him. He got right to the point.

"You're a young man now, Billy," his father told him."You've grown a lot taller in the last six months, and you're still growing. With the miserable amount of relief they give us, you don't have enough to eat. I think you'd be better off to leave school and apply for relief yourself as a single man."

Billy couldn't believe his ears. He'd always planned to become an engineer. Ever since he could remember, he and his dad had talked about how he'd finish school and then go on to university.

Sam Higgins valued knowledge. He was a man who spent a lot of time reading and studying. In the living room there was one whole wall covered with books. They stretched from the floor to the ceiling. Sam was always in there with his nose in one of them, puffing away at his pipe, his feet up on the old red footstool. Yet now he was saying Billy should quit school.

His father explained it all carefully. He always did this so you'd understand why he'd asked you to do something. "These are hard times, Billy. And in hard times you sometimes have to grow up a bit faster than normal. If you ask for relief on your own, you'll at least be getting food enough to grow on. We can't go on as we're doing now."

Then for a long while Sam was quiet. He just sat there and dragged on his pipe. Billy noticed that his father's hair had a lot more grey in it than it used to have.

"There are a million Canadians now without work," Sam went on in a serious voice. "The whole country's caught in this damn Depression. Someone will have to do something soon."

Billy nodded his head vigorously. "That's just what I told Mum," he said. "But what can *we* do?"

"The Depression is worldwide, son. It's all in the hands of the government."

"Then can't the government do something about it?" Billy got up from the chair. He felt frustrated, almost angry. "Don't you think they should, Dad? It's just not fair that we should have to live like this."

"I agree it's not fair, and it's not as though we're asking for miracles either. All we want is a chance to work and earn a living. But I don't know if the government or anybody else can do anything about it."

When Billy kissed his parents goodnight, his father said to him, "Things will improve, Billy, and I'll do everything I can to help you get back to your studies. That's a promise."

That night, as he lay in his bed, Billy's mind was full of so many things. Helen, in her own bed on the other side of the room, was fast asleep; he could tell that from the sound of her breathing, deep and regular. Over and over in his head Billy kept hearing his father's voice: *"You're a young man now, Billy. I think you'd be better off to apply for relief as a single man."*

He thought about growing up and becoming a man. Inside he still felt the same as he'd felt the day before but he knew everything had changed. Even the way his father had talked to him that night had been different. He hadn't talked to him the way he normally did. But more as though Billy were a friend, another man.

Billy went over all the things his father had said about the Depression and everyone being out of work, about leaving school and applying for relief on his own. *"As a single man."* That's what his father had said. A single man! Billy had never thought of himself in that way before. It made him feel a bit afraid.

3

52½ Cordova

THE very day after his birthday Billy's father took him down to 52½ Cordova Street.

52½ Cordova was the headquarters for all the unemployed workers in Vancouver. If anyone without a job had trouble getting food or a place to sleep, he'd go down to Cordova Street and there would be someone to help him.

On the way down on the bus, Sam told Billy how the relief system worked. Married men took their sacks and lined up once a week at the local relief office for their familys' food, but it was different for single men.

"Single men get a daily ticket that's good for a place to sleep and a couple of hot meals," Sam explained. "I've been talking to some of the men at the headquarters. You're young, but I think they'll take you and help you get relief on your own."

Billy listened carefully as his father told him how sometimes, instead of being given money for their bed and board, single unemployed men were sent to relief camps up in the bush. These camps had been set up about three years earlier by the Department of National Defence. Thousands of young single men on relief were sent to the camps. They were given work clothes, a bunk, three meals, and twenty cents a day in return for eight hours work building roads and airports. Billy wondered what his chances were of being sent to the camps, but since he didn't want to upset his father, he didn't ask.

Sam wanted to be sure that Billy understood the situation. Twenty cents a day was not a proper wage, he pointed out. And men resented being isolated away in the bush. So they had formed a union to try to make some changes.

The Relief Camp Workers' Union was organized like a real trade union, but there was one important difference. A trade union is an organization of workers who have jobs, while the Relief Camp Workers' Union was a union of *unemployed* workers.

Billy knew about trade unions. A few years earlier, in an effort to fight wage cuts, Sam had tried to get a union going at the machine shop where he worked. When Mr. Robertson had found out about it, he had talked to most of his employees personally to make it clear to them that he didn't want a union in his shop. He said that a union would make enemies of him and his workers and he liked things the way they were. Most of the tool and dye workers were afraid of losing their jobs. When the time came to vote whether or not to unionize the shop, almost all of them backed down and said no. Only Sam and three other men had continued to fight for the union. And they'd almost been fired over it.

"The Relief Camp Union is working out of Cordova Street, too," Sam told Billy, "so you'll probably meet some of the men."

It was just after nine o'clock in the morning when Sam and Billy got to 52½ Cordova . Even at that hour the comings and goings made it look like a bus terminal on a holiday weekend.

Billy was glad his dad had come with him. He felt a little sick to his stomach from nervousness. What if all the men laughed at him for being such a young kid trying for relief? Worse, what if they got mad at him for trying to get money, thinking he didn't have the same right to it as men who had been working for dozens of years? He tried to act casual and stood a little taller as he walked. To his relief, none of the groups of men, talking and smoking, took any notice of him at all.

There was a poker game going on in one corner. Four men were perched on their haunches around some cards and a pile of matches. Billy was fascinated when one of the players kept "upping the kitty." He pushed the betting higher and higher. Of course, there was no money in this game, but there was a tremendous pile of matches in the middle.

From the looks of the other men, Billy could tell that this character called Jack was making them nervous. They kept watching him carefully. Jack's face wore a serious look and he'd think very hard before making each bet.

Finally, the other men all threw in their cards. Jack let out a "Whoopee" and scooped in all the matches. Billy could see that all along Jack had been bluffing. Instead of the good poker hand that everyone thought he had, Jack had only a miserable pair of twos! He had fooled them all.

Jack's trick was a pretty neat one, Billy thought. He would try it at home on Helen. If he could bluff her, she'd be furious. Helen loved to win all the games she played.

There was no time to stand around watching the poker game. Sam led Billy into one of the small offices, where a wiry man in a red-checked flannel shirt was talking on two telephones at once. When he finished both conversations, he shook Sam's hand. "So this is Billy, eh? Glad to meet you, son. Welcome to the ranks." He shook Billy's hand hard and smiled at him. "I'm going to send McGooley down with him to Employment," he said to Sam. "He'll take good care of the kid and show him the ropes."

Then he yelled out, "McGooley!" at the top of his voice, and Jack McGooley came to the door. He was the ace poker player Billy had been watching outside.

Jack McGooley was older than most of the men around the Cordova Street headquarters. His face was long, with deep furrows on either side of his mouth. His head was bald except for a strip of grey around the back, above his neck. The eyes below the bushy grey brows were a piercing blue, and though they glinted with the devil, they looked kind of sad at the same time. A bit like a clown's eyes, Billy thought.

Billy was pleased it was Jack McGooley who was going down to the employment office with him. As they walked down there, Jack explained how the set-up worked.

"There's nothing to it, Bill. First you register for a job. The guy behind the counter asks how old you are and all that stuff. Then he gets these long sheets and looks to see what jobs are available." McGooley shook his head. "He always looks at the sheets," he added, shrugging his shoulders. "But there's never a damn thing offering. So then he gives you a piece of paper and you go on over to the relief office. They give you vouchers for your bed and board and tell you to come back next week.

"Just one thing I ought to warn you about, Billy," Jack dropped his voice a bit. "Don't say you're still livin' at home. If they know that, they're likely to give you a hard time. Tell 'em you had to move out." Jack said the words very clearly.

"But will I really have to? I mean... will I have to move out?" Billy asked anxiously, feeling he might never get to go home again.

"Don't worry, m'boy. As long as you've got a home

to go to, I'll see you get there. I wouldn't want you to have to spend your nights in some old flea-bag like I've often done," Jack told him. "They take your relief vouchers, then put you in a room with one double bed and three other men like yourself to share it." Jack McGooley's mouth looked grim and determined.

"Really? You've had to sleep four in a bed?" Billy asked.

"Yep. You lie sideways," Jack said with a laugh.

Billy felt his heart beating like a jackhammer inside him when he went up to the wicket. A tired man in glasses looked at him without interest. "I'm looking for a job," Billy said, his voice cracking under the strain. He sounded like a little kid and felt himself blush under his freckles when he told the man his age. The man didn't seem surprised. He got out some forms, and the interview went just as Jack had said it would. By the time the city hall clock struck eleven, Billy had his vouchers for food and accommodation for the next seven days.

"Congratulations, Bill. Now you're an out-of-work bum like the rest of us." Jack put his arm around Billy's shoulders and laughed out loud. Billy tried to smile, too.

The truth was Billy wasn't feeling too happy. In fact, he was feeling quite unhappy. He'd never been all that crazy about going to school, but right at that minute he was missing his classroom and all his old friends. More than anything else he wished that he could see Alfie and tell him all the things that had happened to him since yesterday.

Jack sensed what was going on inside Billy. Suddenly his clown's face lit up. "How about a show, Billy boy, to celebrate your first day as an unemployed worker?"

Billy loved movies. Jack said that the Marx Brothers' *A Night at the Opera* was on at the Rex.

"But I haven't got fifteen cents to get in," Billy remembered. And his face grew long again.

"I haven't got it either," Jack told him with a grin. "But we won't let a little thing like that stop us, will we?"

Jack outlined his plan. Billy listened carefully. Then they went to work. They split up outside the Blue Bird Restaurant. Jack left Billy there and went on up the street to the Rainbow Café.

Billy felt a bit strange about all of this, but Jack had assured him there wasn't a thing to worry about. Perhaps because Billy looked so lost and awkward, the very first person that went into the restaurant asked him if he could help him.

"I wondered, sir, if you could spare fifteen cents for me to buy breakfast," Billy stammered.

The man looked at him for a minute and then said, "I've got a better idea. Why don't you come in with me and we'll have breakfast together."

Billy didn't know what to say to that. He looked up the street, hoping to see Jack, but there was no sign of McGooley.

"Come on, son. You look as if you could do with a proper meal." The well-dressed man took Billy's arm, and together they went into the restaurant. It had been ages since Billy had eaten a breakfast like the one they ordered. Two fried eggs sunny-side up, bacon, hash-brown potatoes and hot buttered toast.

The man was very interested in Billy, especially when he heard the boy had had to quit school and go on relief. "As things are now, it might happen to us all," he said in a quiet voice.

When they'd finished breakfast he slipped two dimes into Billy's hand. "Keep it. It might come in handy," he told him.

Outside the restaurant Billy had to wait for a while for Jack to turn up. When he did appear, he winked at Billy. "Looks like you got a good meal into you."

When the boy showed him the twenty cents as well, Jack roared with laughter. "Not bad for a beginner, m'boy. Not bad at all."

Then Jack told Billy what had happened to him. He'd been offered breakfast too. After the meal he tried again to get his fifteen cents for the movie. The second person he stopped also insisted on buying him breakfast .

So Jack had eaten his second helping of bacon and eggs. Well fed but still without his money for the show, he once more asked someone for fifteen cents for breakfast. When this person offered to buy him bacon and eggs, Jack had to say, "It's so long since

I've eaten properly that my stomach is painin'. Though I think I'll probably be able to face it in an hour or two." So the man had given him fifteen cents!

Billy and Jack laughed for a long time about all of this. Even the Marx Brothers didn't seem any funnier to Billy than his own life was getting to be.

4

On Strike

      · EVERYTHING was very different for Billy once he left school. Suddenly people treated him as an adult. Instead of "Billy, have you done this yet?" or "Billy, how many times do I have to tell you...," now they just counted him in as another pair of hands and expected him to do a good job. And, of course, he did!

He spent most of his time helping out down at 52½ Cordova Street. There was always work to do there. He'd deliver copy for the weekly newspaper. He'd hand out leaflets about a meeting of unemployed workers. Or he'd paste up posters announcing a play or a concert being put on in some union hall. Sometimes he'd go with the other men to stand picket around a house where the landlord was trying to evict a family who couldn't pay their rent.

He made new friends, and some of the jobs were a lot of fun. He certainly was seeing more of the world than if he were sitting behind a desk at school, but his temper began to boil at the thought of the way he had to live. Out of school, picking up nickels and dimes here and there, playing tricks on shopkeepers to save a few pennies — what kind of a future was there in that? And yet a lot of people, grown men, too, had to live the same way, or even worse. Again Billy wondered: Why couldn't something be done about it? Why couldn't someone in charge figure out how to make things work better? Something had to be done about it!

One morning when he went down to the hall at Cordova Street, the activity there was even wilder than usual. Jack grabbed his arm excitedly. "The relief camp workers are going out on strike, and we've got to find beds for them all here in the city. The first batch are expected in tonight."

Billy already knew a bit about the camps around the province. Each time he went to get his relief vouchers, he half expected they might send him to a camp, too. You never knew who would be sent or when they might decide to send you. He had met a number of men from the relief camps. They all hated being locked away out in the middle of nowhere, but even more they hated being paid only twenty cents for a full day's work. No one could see how it was ever going to change.

"We want proper work and wages," they had complained. No one seemed to have listened. Now they were going to go on strike to get it!

Billy and Jack went to every church and union hall they could find, looking for space to bunk down the striking camp workers. Most people were happy to help. By that afternoon they'd found sleeping space for about three hundred men.

"It looks pretty good, Jack, don't you think?" Billy asked the older man.

"Pretty good, but still not good enough," Jack answered. "We'll have to start calling on private homes now to see what space they've got."

"We've got a rollaway cot at home," Billy remembered in a flash. "Maybe we can take a striker ourselves."

Mary and Sam were only too happy to share their home with a striking camp worker. "Fancy paying them only twenty cents a day," said Mary crossly. "Why, you need that much to buy a pound of butter. And a whole chicken costs you even more!"

Billy wrote, "Higgins, 24 Cameroon," right at the top of the list, and the very next day a striker was billeted in his home. That's how Steve Everchuk and Billy Higgins became friends.

Steve was just three years older than Billy, as big, stout and blonde as Billy was thin and redheaded. He'd grown up on a farm in Saskatchewan and was an easy-going boy, tending to take things as they came. "No sense worrying," he told Billy. "Just keep going, and get the most fun you can out of life — that's my motto."

As soon as he moved his things into the Higginses'

closed-in porch, he and Billy started talking. Steve said that the farmers, like everyone else, were having a rough time keeping afloat. It was touch and go, he said, whether his own parents would be able to hang on to their farm. Many farms already had been taken over by banks and mortgage companies when the farmers couldn't meet their payments.

Steve had left the farm to go to southern Alberta to harvest sugar beets there. When the season ended, he'd hopped another freight and gone out to the West Coast. "Riding the freights" — that's the way most people travelled in the Thirties. Hardly anyone had money to buy a train ticket. If they were looking for work in another part of the country, they'd simply hop on top of a freight train and go that way. It wasn't the most comfortable way to travel, and sometimes it landed you in jail. But if you didn't have any other way to go, it was usually worth the risk, Steve told Billy.

"Jail's not so bad, if you don't mind the company," he said wryly. "They don't do anything but lock you in. It's a good way to keep you from spending your money."

He had been in British Columbia almost a year now. Half that time he'd spent working up in a camp near Princeton, earning twenty cents a day.

"It wasn't much fun up there," Steve said. "You'd go out each morning into the bush and cut down trees, and when your work was over, there was nothing else to do. Nowhere else to go," he complained. "Just the same thing day after day. So I figured I'd better come down and see the bright lights and the big city. And help with the strike, too, of course," he added with a grin.

Steve joked about the way he travelled around. "A rolling stone gathers no moss, that's what my mother always said." But from the way he talked, Billy guessed his new friend was really homesick for his farm and the prairies.

Fortunately, there wasn't much time to sit and brood about anything because the minute the strikers hit the streets of Vancouver, that city became the liveliest place in the whole country. Billy, Jack and several hundred others fell in behind that first group of camp workers when they marched through the downtown. It was quite a sight. Men, women and children lined the streets to cheer them on.

Many of the marchers wore the heavy work boots, the grey cloth trousers and the green-brown sweaters that workers were issued in the relief camps. At the head of the parade two men carried a hand-painted banner with the words WE WANT WORK AND WAGES.

Billy watched the men in front of him and tried to keep in step with them. Then he glanced at Jack beside him. He did a little skip to stride out with his left foot at the same time Jack did. It wasn't easy. There was hardly a row where the marchers were in step with one another.

One of the strikers had started to play his accordion, and within minutes the lines of men were singing at the tops of their voices. Billy had never heard the song before, but the melody was easy to follow and he picked up the words from the men around him.

It was a wonderful marching song. Before long the columns of men were striding out together, singing in unison:

> "Hold the Fort for we are coming
>   Union men be strong!
> Side by side we'll battle onward
>   Victory will come!"

"I like this," Billy said to Jack between choruses. "It feels good to do something besides sit around and collect relief. *Now* we're getting somewhere."

"I guess so," Jack said with a wry smile. "The thing of it is, Bill, we haven't got much other choice, now do we?"

5

Strike on the Head

IT took several days before all the strikers from bush camps around the province had arrived in Vancouver. Once they were there, the first big problem was how to feed them.

The Ottawa government said that if the men wouldn't stay in the camps, then there wouldn't be any relief money for them. The B.C. government said that the whole business had nothing to do with them. The mayor and the city council in Vancouver claimed the men weren't their responsibility. The strikers had to take care of themselves.

They applied for permission to hold a tag day to raise money, but Mayor Gerry McGeer said a very definite no. The more than five hundred strikers, needing to be fed some way, held the tag day in spite of the mayor's refusal.

Dozens and dozens of men with tin cans fanned out

over the whole city, collecting nickels and dimes. Billy and Steve were sent out to New Westminster, not far from Robertson's Machine Shop where Sam Higgins had worked for so many years. The shop was all boarded up and looked useless and abandoned.

Almost everyone on the streets gave generously. Men and women dug deep into their pockets and their purses, adding whatever they could to the growing piles of coins in the tin cans. They all knew about the strike. Every newspaper in the province carried headlines an inch high about it.

Sometimes, though, there was an exception.

"What's it for this time, boy?" The man who asked this of Billy was wearing a black hat and carrying a walking stick.

"It's for the unemployed workers, sir. The ones from the relief camps who are on strike," Billy told him.

"And what do they hope to do here in Vancouver?" the man asked.

"We want to talk to the government about getting proper work and wages," Billy replied.

"The government's got more to do than waste its time on a bunch of lazy good-for-nothings," the man said angrily. "If they wanted a job badly enough, they'd stay there in those camps and work." By this time the man's face was very red, and he kept banging his walking stick on the pavement.

"But you can't expect any man to live in the bush month after month and earn only twenty cents a day. It's not right. It's...it's inhuman," Billy protested.

It was what Steve and the other camp workers had told him.

"Inhuman, is it, you young whipper-snapper? The likes of you would be better off in school than panhandling on the streets."

"I'm not panhandling. And I *had* to leave school. We didn't have enough to eat," Billy yelled at him.

"Your parents are the ones to blame. But what can you expect from people who'd rather take a tin can and beg than do an honest day's work." And with this he turned his back on Billy and began to walk away.

At his suggestion that Billy's parents were lazy good-for-nothings, the boy saw red.

"Why, you old...," Billy sputtered. Then, in his back pocket, he felt the slingshot Helen had given him. He put down the tin can, picked up a stone from the gutter, loaded the slingshot, and, with a deadly aim, knocked off the man's black bowler hat.

The man stopped in his tracks and felt his bare head. He turned around and saw Billy with his slingshot. "You vandal! You hooligan!" he shouted as he came forward, puffing with effort, and brought his walking stick down hard on Billy's head.

Everything around Billy started to swim in circles. He saw Steve coming toward him. He saw the blue sky wheeling around. Then he caught a glimpse of the man in the black hat talking to a policeman. The next thing he knew, he was being hustled into a police car.

They took him to the local lock-up and put him in a cell with about thirty other men. His head felt like

lead, and he could feel a bump on it the size of an egg. Now he was in big trouble, and no mistake. His mother had warned him about his temper, and now look where it had got him: locked up with a bunch of criminals. As his head cleared, he remembered what his friend Steve had said about jails, and he looked around him. The men there didn't look very dangerous. In fact, they looked a lot like the men he had met at the Cordova Street office, poorly dressed, but not unfriendly. He soon discovered that they, too, had been tagging on the streets.

The floor and the walls of the cell were made of cement. On the side where the door was, there were iron bars. So many men were crowded in together that they hardly had room to sit down.

"They keep bringin' us in, sayin' we don't have a permit to tag," one of the men told him with a cackle. "But for every fifty of us they lock up, there's another hundred waitin' to go out with their cans. They can't win." And he cackled again, showing a mouthful of rotten teeth.

Around noon there was a terrible commotion in the police station. It was hard to tell exactly what was going on. Then Jack McGooley appeared at the door of the cell with the police sergeant.

"There could be a lot of trouble about this," Jack was saying in a serious voice. "You've got no right to hold a kid like him. He's a minor and has no business being locked up with hardened criminals."

The policeman was clearly confused. "But...we

had no idea," he began.

"Just make sure it doesn't happen again," Jack said to him. "We've got laws in this country to protect our youth."

And with a wink at the men still in the cell, Jack pushed Billy ahead of him out into the sunshine.

Steve was waiting for them in front of the police station. He grinned broadly to see Billy. When he heard how Jack had embarrassed and flustered the police sergeant because of Billy's age, he doubled up with laughter.

"I had that policeman quaking in his boots!" howled Jack. "Of course, I didn't have my tin can with me at the time. I was Mr. Upstanding Citizen himself!"

For a good five minutes the three of them sat down on the curb. They laughed so hard that a passing truck slowed down, and the driver, a big red-faced man wearing a blue bandana, yelled out, "You guys all right?"

They waved him on, tears of laughter in their eyes.

"We're doing just fine," Jack called out. Then they picked themselves up and walked to the closest busy intersection to start collecting money again.

By eight o'clock the word came from Cordova Street that $5,000 had been collected. Five thousand dollars! It was a small fortune! That much money would feed the strikers for quite a few days. But how were they to keep all that money safe until the next day when they could put it in the bank?

Someone had a fine idea. A call was made to the

chief of police, and in short order a police car, its lights flashing, drew up in front of 52½. Two burly policemen got out of the car and lumbered into the strikers' headquarters. All night the two men in the blue uniforms stood guard over the table where the $5,000 lay counted and stacked in a neat pile of tin boxes, each one locked by a tiny key.

It was late when Steve and Billy got back to the little wooden house on Cameroon Street. Sam brewed them all a cup of tea, and Mary made an ice pack to put on Billy's head.

"I knew you'd end up in trouble with the police," she said sharply, but somehow Billy felt she wasn't as angry as she sounded. "That temper of yours, didn't I tell you it would get you in Dutch?"

"Now, Mum, I was completely innocent."

"Oh, indeed. And that's what they all say." She dabbed a scratch with iodine. "Well, I guess you're satisfied now that you're a jailbird. Are you going to tell us what happened or not?"

"I wish you could have seen the look on that policeman's face," Billy told them. "Jack's there giving him a real talking-to, and the guy's face is all puckered up wondering whose side Jack is on."

Billy was acting out all the roles in his story as if it were a play in a theatre. The more everyone laughed, the more he'd strut around like the burly, confused police sergeant or like Jack McGooley making a fool of the other man.

Only later when Helen cornered him alone in the

living room was Billy forced to tell the other side of the story.

"Weren't you scared when they put you in jail?" she asked him.

"It wasn't that bad," he said, shrugging his shoulders.

"Not even a little bit scared?" Helen insisted, putting her face right up close to his.

"Well...maybe a little bit," Billy admitted at last. "The worst thing was feeling trapped in there behind those bars. And I didn't know how I'd ever get out."

"I would have come to visit you every day," Helen said earnestly. "But I'm awfully glad they let you go," she added softly, putting her hand in his.

"I'm glad too. At home I've only got to share a room with you, but in jail there were about thirty of us there jammed in the same cell." This last remark he added with a grin, giving his sister's hand a little squeeze as he said it.

When they finally went to bed, Billy was asleep in minutes. He didn't hear the bedroom door open softly, and he didn't see his mother steal in quietly and sit down in the rocking chair. He had no idea she spent most of the night there, watching him and rocking slowly.

The room was dark except where a sliver of moonlight shone in through the window. Even if Billy had seen his mother sitting there, he probably wouldn't have been able to tell that her cheeks were wet with tears.

6

Gone Fishin'

THERE wasn't much time in those hectic weeks for Billy to show Steve around the city; yet there were so many things he wanted his friend to see. It only stands to reason that when you live in a city, you get to know it in a very special way. You learn its secrets, things that visitors rarely ever find out by themselves.

Billy, for instance, knew a spot to fish that was almost magic. It was down the creek that was behind Alfie Baker's uncle's place. No matter what time of the day it was or what season of the year, you always had a few bites there. Usually, you'd take home five or six perch, and sometimes, if you were especially lucky, even a trout or two.

Billy badly wanted to take Steve fishing there, but the first month after the strikers arrived in Vancouver was so busy that there was just no time. Then one afternoon when there was nothing much happening in the streets, the two boys decided to take the afternoon off and catch what they could for dinner.

It was already the middle of May. Each day now the sun was higher in the sky, and you could tell again what summer would be like.

Billy brought along his rod and the flat green box with his gear. His new fly was in the box, still bright and shiny. He'd been so busy since his birthday he hadn't had a chance to use it yet. Steve carried Sam's good rod. They walked down by old Harry Tomlin's chicken shed and then turned left and followed the road past the school. Everyone was in class. Things seemed quiet around the red brick building.

Billy told Steve about his school days there, about his friend Alfie, and about Alfie's uncle Frank. Frank Baker was the best fisherman Billy had ever known. He seemed to have some kind of sixth sense that let him know where the fish were biting.

The boys were going to step in and say hello to Frank and ask how Alfie was doing on the reserve. But when they got to the rambling old shack where Frank lived, the place was all boarded up. No one seemed to be living there. A barbed wire fence stood all around the shack. The sharp wire strands stretched even beyond the old grey building and ran for several hundred yards along the side of the creek. A black sign with red letters said: "Keep out. Trespassers will be prosecuted."

Billy couldn't understand it. Although he hadn't been down to the creek for months, he'd had no idea Frank had moved away. It seemed odd to Billy. He wondered what could have made Frank leave his home and where he might have gone.

The path down to the creek was blocked by the barbed wire. Billy ran up a little to see if farther along there was another way down. It was impossible. The creek bank rose sharply, and there was a sheer drop down to the water.

The boys kept walking along the road to where an old concrete bridge spanned the water. On one side of the bridge they managed to slide down to the creek bank.

They put their things under a drooping willow tree. The long, new green leaves moved gently around them in the warm air, making striped patterns on the surface of the water. Steve and Billy set their lines carefully with the cork floats, the sinkers, traces, and the wiggling fat worms stuck as bait on to the sharp hooks. Then they made themselves comfortable and settled down to wait.

"Do you miss not going to school, Billy?" Steve asked.

Billy shook his head. "I've learned more things these past three months than I could ever have learned in school," he said.

"But we can't always go on like this," Steve told him. "Some of the guys with me in the Princeton camp have been without work now for five years.

Some of them have never had a steady job in their lives. One fella wanted to get married, but there was no way he could without a job or even the hope of getting one."

"I thought you were the one who thought the best way to live is to drift around and have fun," Billy said.

"It's okay for a time," smiled Steve. "But a fella's got to grow up someday."

Billy didn't answer. He pulled his line out of the water and checked the hook and the bait. Everything was in place, so he let it down again. It made a little plop as it fell through the water. That, the occasional croaking of the frogs along the banks of the creek, and the movement of the wind through the trees were the only sounds that could be heard.

Billy felt impatient and restless, though he knew from experience that these were terrible qualities in a fisherman. Nothing about the afternoon had gone the way he'd planned. He'd talked so much to Steve about this creek and the great fun he and Alfie and Alfie's uncle Frank used to have here. Now nothing was the same. He wondered why Frank had gone away and why the shack was all fenced off like that. It certainly wasn't the kind of thing Frank would have done himself, Billy felt sure.

The fishing wasn't going well either. Steve got only one bite, and when his line came up out of the water, there was no fish straining on the end of it. The fish had got away, taking Steve's bait with it. Billy didn't even get a nibble!

The boys packed up their gear to go home. As they passed the grey shack again, Billy looked carefully for some sign that might tell him what had happened or where Frank Baker might have gone. The only moving object around the house was a loose board over one of the windows. It kept flapping in the wind, making a blunt, loud clap each time it came down again.

Then Billy caught a glimpse of a black cat skulking along the edge of the shack. "Midnight. Psst, Midnight," he called urgently.

But the scrawny cat seemed afraid of him. She arched her back and narrowed her green eyes before darting nervously toward the bushes down by the creek.

The cat's presence puzzled Billy more than ever. Midnight and Frank had lived together in the shack for a long time. He could hardly believe Frank would have gone away and left the cat there alone.

As they walked back along the dirt road to Cameroon Street, Steve asked Billy what he thought might have happened to Frank Baker. Billy just shrugged his shoulders. He didn't feel much like talking.

7

Marching on the Bay

ALL the unemployed in Vancouver had joined the striking camp workers. Together they were trying to explain to people that something had to change. Canadian workers needed work to do. They wanted to do something useful and earn a living wage. It was becoming clear, though, that no one in government wanted to talk to them. No one wanted to take responsibility for the thousands of unemployed workers walking the streets of Vancouver. The city said it had nothing to do with them. The province blamed the federal government in Ottawa. And Ottawa didn't say a thing.

The unemployed didn't give up. Since they knew it was important to have the support of as many Canadians as possible, they held meetings, picnics, marches and demonstrations of all kinds in every corner of the city. They even marched into Woodward's and Spencer's department stores. There were so many shoppers inside that within five minutes the men had marvellous audiences. They explained why they were on strike and what they wanted from the government. "Support us," they asked the people in the stores, and some of them looked as if they would.

It was all very exciting. However, the store owners became nervous. Fearing that all these unemployed workers marching through their stores would be bad for business, they called the police. Within minutes the strikers were out on the streets again.

Before they were thrown out, a newspaper reporter had time to get a picture of the men talking to the shoppers. The picture hit the front page the very next morning and was great publicity for the strike. After this episode, policemen guarded all the entrances to the big department stores.

The unemployed workers were divided into three divisions. Every morning each division would take a different part of the city, and the men would march to their appointed areas, singing and shouting their slogans.

Billy, Steve and Jack McGooley were all in Division Three. One morning their division marched west on Hastings Street. At Granville they turned south and kept going to the corner of Georgia.

"We want work and wages! We want work and wages!" they chanted. "Down with the slave camps! Work and wages!"

The marching men swung east on Georgia and

then turned again at Seymour Street. When they got abreast of the entrance to the Hudson's Bay department store, the men leading the march noticed there were no guards at the door. It was too good an opportunity to miss. The first rows of marchers turned into the store entrance. Row after row of the unemployed workers followed them in.

For a few minutes they marched and chanted around the main floor. Most of the shoppers looked amused; one or two even began to applaud. The leader of the division gave a speech. Then one of the other men spoke for a few minutes about the relief camps. He said they ought to be closed down. "Canadians need proper work to do. And at decent wages," he added.

There was another round of applause. Jack McGooley caught Billy's eye and winked at him. Everything had gone off very well. The men were in good spirits.

"All right, you guys, get into formation again! We're heading back to Cordova Street."

The men responded quickly. They began to form into lines, four men to a line. At that very moment a unit of blue uniforms swept through the main doors of the store. Each policeman carried a billy club in his hand. There must have been a hundred of them. Within seconds they were on top of the strikers, and a free-for-all broke out!

Shoppers and strikers alike made a dash for the doors, only to find that all entrances to the store were blocked. They hid behind showcases and under counters, wherever they could find shelter, but it wasn't easy to avoid those swinging clubs.

The strikers were furious. They fought back with whatever they could find. Before long the whole main floor of the store was in shambles.

Billy and Steve managed to get between a group of life-size mannequins dressed in the latest summer fashions. "I don't think your shirt is quite the right colour for this season's styles," Billy managed to yell before they both dived again for the door.

Outside, several of the other strikers were being bundled into a paddy wagon. The door was slammed after them, and the vehicle sped off down the street.

"You boys alright?" It was Jack asking, his face streaked with blood. He looked a mess. "They nearly got us that time," he told the men.

With the wide grin on his long, tired face and the blood streaming from a cut above one eye, Jack looked more than ever like a tragic clown.

There wasn't time to stand there talking. The streets around the store had filled with people. Divisions One and Two had heard about the fiasco in the Hudson's Bay store and had rushed over — but not only the strikers had come. It looked to Billy as if the whole of Vancouver had got wind of what had happened and had all come down to help.

For a few minutes there was such confusion in the street that no one seemed to know what to do. Then suddenly the police were there among the crowds.

The fighting that had gone on inside the store spread now to the streets.

"Get over to Victory Square," yelled a burly fellow in a blue peaked cap. "They're bringing Mayor McGeer down to talk to us."

Getting to Victory Square wasn't easy. Several times Billy lost Jack and Steve in the crush. Twice he tripped and almost fell under the feet of the men and women running toward the square. He felt the edge of panic as he tried to keep up. Out of breath, the three finally managed to reach their destination. It was hard to move, there were so many people, but they managed to shove their way closer to the centre of the square, with Jack leading the way, elbowing his way through. Soon they were near the memorial to the Canadian soldiers who had died in the First World War.

A big black car drew up, flanked by policemen on motorcycles. The mayor got out and was rushed to the centre of the square. There, on the steps of the cenotaph, Mayor McGeer read the riot act. He asked that all the people in the streets go back immediately to their homes. If not, he would ask the police to get rid of them.

By this time there must have been several thousand men and women gathered there. They looked around at each other, uncertain what to do. Every single one of them was painfully aware of the policemen moving into the streets surrounding Victory Square.

There were Mounties wearing steel helmets like soldiers, provincial policemen with guns, and city police with billy clubs gripped tight in their fists. Some of the police rode horses, and the big, handsome animals stamped their feet nervously, restless among the crowds.

For just a few minutes there was an uneasy, ugly silence in the square. Then gradually, men and women started to turn and file slowly through the rows of policemen back to their homes.

Billy was confused, but he was angry too, so angry he wanted to cry. He felt like a little boy again, in trouble with the principal at school. But this was different. It wasn't school and the mayor wasn't the principal. This was serious. He looked at Steve and Jack. Their faces were grim. The blood on Jack's face had dried now and streaked down to his chin in thin red lines. Not one of them said a word. Finally, they too turned and moved out of the square.

8

An Important Decision

AS the days stretched into weeks, a feeling of terrible frustration hung over Vancouver. Down at 52½ Cordova Street the men seemed to have lost all of their energy. Even Jack, who could usually liven the place up with a few stories or a poker game, was quiet.

The strikers had tried everything they could think of to force the government to talk to them, but they were getting nowhere. They continued holding their meetings, collecting money and handing out leaflets. With no results, they knew they couldn't continue this way for much longer.

One day toward the end of May when Billy was walking down Hastings in the direction of Cordova, he noticed a group of men outside a store. There was a big sign in the store window. The green cardboard was lettered roughly in pencil: "Wanted — Experienced Salesman." All around the sign were electrical cords, plugs, lightbulbs, a couple of faded lampshades, even an electric toaster that looked as if it had stood there for two or three years waiting for someone to buy it. Everything in the window was covered with thick dust. Everything except the green cardboard sign.

As Billy stood looking, an old man climbed awkwardly among the lightbulbs and the cords and plugs. He stepped carefully over the faded lampshades and the dusty toaster, picked up the sign and took it with him out of the window.

A couple of the men standing glumly in front of the store shook their heads and walked away. Most of the others did not even seem to notice the sign was gone now. It was almost as if they had never expected it to change much for them anyway.

Then Billy recognized a familiar figure sitting on the edge of the sidewalk. The big man was sitting there with his head in his arms. His cap was almost falling off his head, and the old jacket he wore had a big tear across the back.

"Frank, hey Frank, what are you doing here?" Billy shook the man's arm.

Frank Baker opened his dark eyes and squinted at Billy as he sat upright.

"Oh, it's you, Billy. Been a long time since I've seen you," he said in a low voice, his eyes looking over the boy's face. Then Frank looked away and stared blankly into space.

Billy sat down beside the big figure on the side of the curb. "What happened at the house, Frank. Why did you leave?" he asked him.

"Oh that," Frank said, shrugging his shoulders. "The trust company that owns the land down there, they said I had to get out 'cause I had no money to pay them the rent. Can't imagine that old shack is worth much to them, can you?" Frank looked right at Billy, his brown eyes filling up with tears.

Billy had never seen Frank cry. He didn't like to see him crying now.

"Why don't you go somewhere and get help?" Billy asked him. "I know a place where..."

"Forget it, Billy," Frank broke in. "Nothing you can do when those big guys get after you. Nothing at all you can do."

Frank kept looking in front of him as if he were seeing something far, far away. Billy couldn't tell what that might be because the expression on Frank's face didn't change even the least little bit. Then without turning his head, Frank said, "Too bad we can't go fishin' anymore down the creek, Billy."

After he'd said that, Frank put his head down on his arms again as if he were going to sleep right there on the edge of the sidewalk.

"Hey Frank," Billy pulled at the worn jacket. "Frank, you can't sleep here. Come with me."

However much he called and tugged, the big figure wouldn't budge. Billy looked around at the other men to see if one of them might help him. Most of them had moved off down the street. Only one man was left standing by himself with his hands in his pockets, leaning against the window where the green cardboard sign had been. He didn't seem to hear Billy when the boy called to him, and Billy thought the man was not really there at all. His eyes were fixed on something distant in the way Frank's had been.

The boy sat down on the curb beside the sleeping man. For a long time he sat there, hoping Frank might wake up again, but Frank looked as if he could sleep for hours yet. Finally, Billy got up and walked slowly away.

By the time he reached Cordova Street, Billy's spirits were very low. On the sidewalk outside the hall, he met Jack. He was going to tell him about seeing Frank down on Hastings Street, but Jack seemed to have news of his own. The long, furrowed face was wreathed in smiles.

"What's up, Jack? You just won the sweepstakes or something?" Billy asked him.

"Even better than that, Billy m'boy," Jack answered happily. "I'm plannin' to take a little trip. I'm off to Ottawa to meet personally with the prime minister. Wanna come too?"

Jack explained. At a meeting that morning someone had suggested that since the government wouldn't come to talk to the strikers, the strikers should go to Ottawa to talk to the government.

"On to Ottawa, boys," shouted Jack, waving his fist in the air. "On to Ottawa! Are you with us, Billy?"

"Am I!" At last, thought Billy, something was going to be done. He thought of the jail, and of how his father hated not having a job. He thought of Frank Baker's despair and hopelessness, and the way things just seemed to keep slipping from bad to worse. Did he want to spend the rest of his life fighting in the streets and using a slingshot to pick off the bowler hats of old men? What about his education, his hopes for the future? He punched Jack in the arm. "Count me in, partner," he said.

It took several days before the plans were finalized. The pros and cons of going to meet with Prime Minister R. B. Bennett and his government were discussed in groups all over the city.

"What's the use going to talk to Bennett?" some of the men asked. "He's a Tory and a millionaire. He won't give a damn about the likes of us."

"A Tory or a Grit, it's all the same once they're in Ottawa," some of the others added.

"What's a Tory and a Grit?" Billy asked Jack.

"That's what the Conservatives and the Liberals call each other," Jack told him. "And it's a darn sight more polite than what most of the workers are calling them these days."

"I'm not sure I understand," Billy said, wrinkling up his nose.

"Look, boy, the Liberals were in power for years and years," Jack started again. "Then when things started to go bad and people began losin' their jobs, old Mackenzie King, the Liberal prime minister, swore he wouldn't spend a nickel on unemployment relief. That made people mad. So in 1930 there were new elections and in came the other side. The Tories under Dickie Bennett promised the world. But once he got to be prime minister, Mr. Bennett seemed to forget every word he'd said." Jack's voice sounded disgusted. "Ugh — the way they're in and out without doing anything, they make you feel quite sick, they do," he said, flinging his arms up and down. Billy, watching Jack's arms swinging in the air, was inclined to agree.

In the end, a vote was taken among the unemployed workers in Vancouver. They came to a decision. They would trek across the country to see the prime minister in Ottawa. They would explain their situation and insist that he help them.

Billy rushed home to tell his parents the news. Sam wasn't there and Mary's first reaction wasn't quite what Billy had hoped. "You're much too young to be gallivanting around," she said in a cross voice.

When Sam came home, he already knew about the decision to go to Ottawa. In his quiet voice he told his wife, "The boy has to grow up and come to terms with the world. There's no future for him the way things are now. It's better he goes with the others to try to change things."

Mary didn't argue with him. When Sam got that quiet, reasonable-sounding tone in his voice, they all knew he had come to a decision inside. There was no way of changing his mind.

Billy was very excited — now Steve would get to see the prairies again, and he would get to see Canada. Ottawa, the Parliament buildings, the prime minister!

He couldn't sleep for hours that night thinking about it all. He wondered what the prime minister would look like and if he'd get to talk to Mr. Bennett himself. Billy didn't think he was very good at things like that. He never knew what to say when he had to meet someone new, and if that someone was the *prime minister of Canada*, it would be just that much harder.

On second thought though, maybe it wouldn't be so difficult to find something to say. They were just going to explain to Mr. Bennett how hard things were for them without jobs or enough money to live. When you have something specific to say like that, you don't have to fish around for words.

9

Riding the Freights

THE decision to go to Ottawa gave the unemployed workers their spirits back. June 3 was the date they set to leave Vancouver. When that day rolled around, there was a feeling in the air that something tremendous was happening.

Nearly one thousand strikers lined up at the foot of Gore Street, ready to hop aboard the Canadian Pacific Railway freight when it pulled out shortly after ten at night. As well as those taking part in the On-to-Ottawa Trek, there were at least a thousand more people to see them off.

The freight was a particularly long one. Billy started to count the boxcars and got up to ninety-two, though Helen swore she'd counted only ninety. Everyone was wondering if the police would let them board the train, but there was not a policeman in sight. The men climbed up the iron steps to the roofs of the boxcars and settled themselves down there.

"Hold on, Billy, when it goes fast," his mother called up to him with a worried look on her face.

"And remember to send me a postcard of Niagara Falls!" Helen yelled through cupped hands.

Sam didn't call out anything. Before Billy had climbed aboard, his father had just smiled and pressed two dollars into his hand. Billy knew his father wanted to come too, but almost all the men on the Trek to Ottawa were single unemployed workers. If the married men left home, their families wouldn't get any relief.

Finally, it was time to go. The long train pulled away slowly. Billy and Steve waved and waved until the figures beside the tracks were just tiny specks in the distance.

As the freight inched forward through the dark city, it was cheered on at every crossroad by groups of well-wishers who'd come out to say goodbye. After a half hour or so there were no more city crossroads, no more clusters of lights from neat rows of houses, no more cheering crowds. The train picked up speed.

Billy clutched the iron cat-rail around the side of the boxcar. Each time the train jerked, he was terrified that he'd fall off. He tried to make his body move with the carriage as it gathered a fast, repetitive rhythm.

It was easy to tell which men had ridden the freights before. Some of them wore three layers of clothing to keep themselves warm. They wrapped blankets around their heads, sat with their backs to the engine, and were asleep before the train was an hour out of Vancouver.

Billy propped himself up against his knapsack and tried to do the same, but he didn't feel safe enough up there to allow himself to fall into a deep sleep. Yet he must have dozed off. Several times he came to with a start as the long freight groaned to a stop at some siding. Once or twice he was woken by the icy wind from the Fraser River canyon as it whipped around his head. He tried to pull his cap down over his ears and hunched up his shoulders under the thick, brown blanket his mother had insisted he bring with him.

As the night subsided and the pale pink glow of the dawn crept above the horizon, Billy was wide awake. He watched in fascination as the green countryside sped by him. Apple orchards and pear trees still laden with blossoms passed before his eyes.

People came out of their houses to stare at the train. Most of them waved enthusiastically. Canadians had grown used to seeing freight trains rattling by with men sitting on the sun-warmed steel on top of the cars, but this particular freight was something special. Nearly one thousand men sat swaying on top of it — and all of them were on their way to Ottawa, almost a continent away.

Early in the morning the train made a routine stop for water. The old hands riding on top clambered down the iron steps to stretch their legs. The trekkers were all cold and hungry by this time. There was nothing much around except for a small wooden building beside the tracks. A faded painted sign read: "The Canadian Café." It seemed just the place to buy coffee and doughnuts. The idea caught on fast. As soon as Billy and Steve saw some of the others sipping hot coffee, they were off the train before you could blink your eyes.

Pandemonium reigned in the Canadian Café. The owners had never seen that many customers in the whole history of the place. Doughnuts and cups of coffee sailed through the air, over heads, passing from hand to hand, as the men all tried to get served.

The trekkers kept one ear cocked toward the train to hear when the freight whistle blew. Some of them even got behind the counter and started to help. Billy and Steve managed to get a coffee to share between them mainly because Jack was an old hand at all this. He'd been one of the first off the train and into the café. Billy hated coffee, but at least it was hot and laced with milk and sugar. There were still a few bologna sandwiches tied in the tea towel that Mary Higgins had given Billy. These were passed around and quickly finished.

After an hour, the train whistle sounded, shrill and loud. That was it. Anyone who hadn't managed to get served, missed out. The men climbed quickly aboard again, and off they went.

Trying to feed one thousand hungry, tired men with

little or no money was not an easy task. Some of the trekkers were already beginning to worry about how they would manage for food during the long trip. Billy himself could see problems ahead.

The first real stop of the Trek had been planned for Kamloops. It was nearly noon when the train finally shuddered to a halt. The men climbed down and were quickly organized into lines of four, just as they had been on their marches through Vancouver.

Looking about, they saw that there were no enthusiastic crowds here to welcome them or cheer them on. Just a few of the local people came out, curious to see the crowds of men climbing off the train and marching through their streets on the way to Riverside Park.

Most of the men were silent on that march. When they got to the park, they couldn't see any sign that they'd been expected. No tables of food. No welcomers. The large grounds were empty.

"How are we supposed to eat?" one of the men said to the group around him.

"We'll never make it," grumbled another.

"It's all well and good to say we'll go to Ottawa, but it has to be better planned than this," someone else threw in.

"We might as well pack it all in right here and now. The whole thing is impossible," said another quiet voice.

Billy didn't say anything, not even to Steve. He listened to the men around him, and he certainly understood what they were saying. He felt hungry himself. His muscles were stiff from the long, cold trip on top of the train.

"And this is just the beginning," he thought. They were still in British Columbia. They had to get over the Rockies and then across the prairies of Alberta and Saskatchewan before heading into Manitoba and then, finally, into Ontario.

Though he would never have admitted it, Billy felt homesick. He wondered what his mother and father were doing now. And Helen. Billy would have given anything to see his sister. He'd even take her fishing, he thought, and let her use his new fly.

Billy put his hand in his pocket and around the smooth wood of the slingshot Helen had made him for his birthday. For a minute or two it made her round, smiling face framed in the curly dark hair seem a bit closer to him. But as Billy looked at the tired men standing and grumbling in groups around the park, he realized that Helen wasn't close at all. Helen and Sam and Mary and the familiar little wooden house on Cameroon Street were getting very far away indeed.

Suddenly, from the back of a truck parked in the middle of the grounds, a man called to them through a megaphone. Billy moved up closer to the truck. He recognized Slim Evans standing there. Slim had been one of the most active leaders of the strike in Vancouver. Billy had often seen him around Cordova Street, organizing delegations to city hall or rousing the audience at a public meeting. Now Slim stood alone on top of the truck, asking the men to listen to him.

"I know a lot of you feel disheartened there's been no reception waiting for us here. But remember, Kamloops is our first stop. People aren't used to meeting so many of us at one time. They don't know yet the kind of help we need from them. They don't know how big a movement we've got or what a group this size can do. But they'll learn. And we'll help to teach them."

Slim paused for a few seconds and then went on. "We've worked together for a long time. Don't give up now. We've just begun our biggest battle." He finished his speech by asking, "Now who's for going to Ottawa, and who's for going back?"

The response was deafening. The whole park resounded with whistles and applause and cries of "On to Ottawa! On to Ottawa!"

Billy heard no more grumbling that afternoon. The men organized into divisions as they'd done in Vancouver, and they sent delegations all over the town.

They were only in Kamloops one day, but they held a public meeting, collected money, and managed to put together a meal for all the men. When they got on the train again, there was a different attitude among the trekkers. Now they knew the difficulties that faced them and the need for a good, strong organization. But more than ever they were determined to get to Ottawa and speak to the prime minister.

"We'll show the whole country that it can be done," Billy told Steve, his green eyes shining. "When Mr. Bennett sees us all, he'll just have to help us. I know he will." With that, he pulled his cap low over his forehead and settled down again with his back to the engine.

10

A Golden Welcome

THE long freight train began to snake a path through the canyons leading to the Rocky Mountains. Moonlight and a million twinkling stars lit up the early morning as if it were day.

It was already the end of the first week in June and along the West Coast the days had been warm, but as the train started the long climb through the snow-capped peaks, the air grew bitterly cold.

Billy gazed, speechless, at the towering peaks that seemed to surround them now on every side. While Jack, Steve and most of the other men huddled in their blankets, trying to sleep, Billy's eyes were wide open as he craned his neck to see the new country that he was discovering. He wished Alfie could be with him to see the mountain streams falling hundreds of feet into the valleys below. The two of them could have a great time fishing in those streams.

The engine, chugging through tunnels and mountain passes, spewed black coal smoke into the clean air. The men, their backs to the engine, let their bodies sway loosely as the carriages clattered in monotonous rhythm over the steel tracks.

On the way across the Rockies there were two very long tunnels. One curved through a mountain for seven miles. As the first tunnel loomed nearer, the trekkers crouched down and wrapped their blankets more closely around their heads. It was dark and airless and very uncomfortable inside, and by the time the train came out into the clear night air again, Billy felt sick to his stomach. He closed his eyes and gripped the handrail along the side of the car even more tightly.

"Hey there, Bill, I wouldn't have recognized you," Jack McGooley told him. "With all that black on your face you haven't got a freckle to be seen."

It was true. What was visible of Billy's face under his cap was completely black with coal-dust. There wasn't a brown freckle showing through.

At any other time Billy would have been delighted to hear this. Now, up on top of the freight, he felt too sick to care. He tried to wriggle down and lay his head on the roof of the car, but it was hard to get enough room for that. The men were jammed so tightly together that lying down was out of the question.

"Just lay your head against my shoulder and take a few deep breaths," Jack told him. "It'll pass in a few minutes, you'll see. There's no air in them tunnels. That's what you're sufferin' from."

Billy lay back against Jack's shoulder. He wished he were back home again in his own bed instead of being up there in the cold air, feeling like being sick. He kept his eyes closed tight because whenever he opened them, he felt worse.

Softly, from the other end of the train, he could hear a few quiet notes of music. The isolated notes became gentle chords, and before you knew what was happening, the accordion was playing the old "Hold the Fort." It had become the theme song of the On-to-Ottawa Trek.

A few voices started out singing the words; then a few more joined in. By the end of the first chorus it sounded as if every single man on top of the freight train was singing his heart out:

"Hold the Fort for we are coming
Union men be strong!
Side by side we'll battle onward
Victory will come!"

Billy never knew if it was the music or the clear fresh air that did it, but within a very short time he felt as good as new. He was ready again for whatever might be ahead.

News about the Trek was now spreading like a

forest fire. Nothing like it had ever been tried before. Over breakfast the whole country read their newspapers and listened to their radios to hear where the train was now. What would Mr. Bennett do with this unusual delegation on its way to see him?

After Kamloops everything on the Trek seemed to look up. The next stop was Golden, a town at the eastern edge of British Columbia. It was about five o'clock in the morning when the men got there and were marched out to the park on the banks of the Kicking Horse River.

And what a sight awaited them!

It seemed that every wash tub in the little town was there in the park, filled to the brim with bubbling stew. Billy couldn't believe his eyes. He even saw a full-size bathtub suspended over a glowing fire. A little, old grey-haired woman was stirring it with a ladle three feet long. In the pale morning light he thought he was looking at a good fairy from one of his childhood storybooks.

The warm welcome at Golden provided a great lift to the trekkers. After that it was easy to keep their spirits up, even when the going was rough. Now the men knew they weren't alone.

At every stop along the way, new people would join them. Already there were 1,700 unemployed workers on the Trek to Ottawa. Nobody tried to stop them from getting on and off the freights, and every time they stopped, people were there to meet them, to feed them, to listen to their plans.

Calgary, Medicine Hat, Swift Current, Moose Jaw
— Billy was seeing Canada in a way he'd never forget. And always there was that same tune in the background and a chorus of determined voices singing the words:

"Side by side we'll battle onward
Victory will come!"

11

The Pogey

NOT only was Billy getting to know the country, he was getting to know the trekkers, too. They came from all over the place. There were miners from Cape Breton who had been laid off from their jobs in the coal mines, loggers from northern Ontario and Quebec, farmers like Steve from the Prairies, salesmen and sailors, and men like his dad who'd worked in machine shops and factories. And there were lots of young men only a few years older than himself, who had never had a chance to work much at anything.

A lot of the men had travelled all over Canada and the United States, back and forth across the border, looking for work. Men like Red Walsh, who was a good friend of Jack McGooley. Red was born in the United States, and he spoke with an accent that Jack said was "pure Bronx with a fair smatterin' of Irish."

Billy didn't know if that was right or not, but he did know that Red's accent made everything he said sound bigger than life.

Red was the leader of Division Two. The very first day Jack introduced Billy to him, Red stood for a minute scratching his head, looking the boy up and down. Then he threw back his head and roared.

"God's teeth, kid. My real name is Jim, though no one's ever called me that. I've always been 'Red' 'cause of my freckles and my red hair. But I never had a case of freckles like you got. What d'they call you?" Red laughed again.

Normally Billy hated anyone to mention his freckles. Yet when it was someone like Red, who was himself freckled all over, it was different. There was a kind of bond between them. He grinned and told Red his name.

Red Walsh had started out as a steelworker in Philadelphia. The day Billy asked him when he'd come to Canada, a smile played around the freckled face for a second or two before he answered.

"I come to Canada in 19 and 32. A friend of mine had a sister livin' in Toronto. He was goin' over there to see the sister, and I decided to go with him. My intention was to go to Calgary, Alberta, and go across to Montana in the States and then go home. I hoped to get some sort of work but the Deeee-pression was already on and there was no work. Eventually I went into a relief camp in Alberta."

Red said Deeee-pression as if it were two words.

Billy liked the sound of it said that way. Though when he thought about it for a bit, he realized there was nothing at all to like about the Depression. If there'd been no Depression, his father wouldn't have lost his job. Frank Baker would still be living down near the creek, and Alfie would be there too and...

Red must have seen the thoughtful look that came over Billy's face because he went on quickly with his story.

"I stayed in Alberta about six months. Then I went to Vancouver on a freight train. We just hopped it. Got into an empty boxcar and got off in Vancouver. Always lookin' for a job. But there was no job. No job anywhere! In Vancouver I applied again for relief and they sent me to the pogey."

"The pogey?" questioned Billy with a laugh. It was such a funny-sounding word.

Red nodded his head. "That's what they called it — the pogey. It was a warehouse and they filled it full of bunks. A hundred and fifty men on each of the two floors. The beds were so close together, you couldn't get in between them. The men were frustrated, so we decided we were goin' to get out of there. I drew up a plan of the floor I was on — the doors and the elevator and everything. At the front of the building there was a very large window with wire over it. It was taller than I am and almost as wide as it was tall. I decided the only thing we could do was to throw the beds out the window, onto the street."

When Red told Billy that, the boy was shocked. "If

you really hated this pogey place, why didn't you just leave? It wasn't a jail, was it?" he asked, remembering the trapped feeling he'd had when he'd been put behind bars himself.

"No, Billy, it wasn't a jail," Red told him patiently. "But it might just as well have been. We had to stay there jammed together like sardines or we wouldn't 'ave got a thing to eat."

Billy tried hard to understand what Red was saying. "Then this pogey must have been a bit like the relief camps. You had no choice. Either you stayed there or they'd cut you off relief?" Billy said the words slowly, somehow understanding them better when he said them aloud.

"That's exactly it," Red answered quickly. And he smiled at Billy, nodding his head up and down.

"And just like in the old tar-paper shacks in the camps," Red went on, "you got no sheets or anything in the pogey. A thin blanket was the only cover on the old straw mattress they gave you."

Then in a quiet voice he added, "But the worst part was not seeing an end to it all. We wanted to work but there was nothing for us to do. It seemed we might go on like that for years and years. We knew we had to get out of there."

Red's bright eyes were looking far away now as if he'd forgotten Billy was there right in front of him.

"So what did you do?" Billy asked, raising his voice a bit so Red would remember he was there.

Red jerked his head and tried to remember where

he was in his story. "Well...we threw the beds out the window and they did the same on the floor below."

"Wow," said Billy, trying to imagine so many beds going out of the windows with the wire across them.

"When all the beds were gone off our floor, I looked out and for the first time I saw a Mounted Police. The Royal Canadian Mounted Police with the large hat and the red jacket. Never saw one before in my life."

Red wasn't a very tall man, and as he mentioned the RCMP, his eyes went up, up as if he were looking at a giant from his boots to his wide-brimmed hat. Billy laughed at the thought of little Red and the big Mountie.

Red went on with his story. "All of a sudden the lights went on. I was bleedin' out of the hand. I cut myself with glass, but it wasn't much. The supervisor, he's on the floor shakin' his head. He couldn't understand any of this. He thought he was doin' a wonderful job. Anyway they arrested everybody. They arrested the whole three hundred."

"Did they put you in jail then?" Billy wanted to know.

"They took us up to the police station, and the next morning we were taken before this immigration man. He was a representative of the Immigration Department of Canada." Red made a funny face so that Billy would understand this immigration man was a very important fellow. "We went in one by one. You went in one door and you went out another. You didn't go out the way you came in, otherwise you'd be able to tell the others what was goin' on. So I went in. He asked me my name. I told him.

"'Where were you born?' he asks me.

"'I was born in Nova Scotia,' I say.

"'Is that so? You're a Canadian then?'

"'That's right,' I tell him.

"'How many provinces in Canada?' he asks me.

"'About twelve or thirteen,' I say. I just didn't know at all. But I knew if I owned up I wasn't a Canadian they'd deport me."

"Deport you?" Billy repeated it after Red, uncertain of exactly what it meant.

"They did deport some people out of that pogey. Sent them right back to England and Scotland. To wherever they'd originally come from. Even though those men had been Canadians for years, workin' and livin' here just like all the others that were born here."

"What happened to you?"

"There were so many people involved in this that the public couldn't get into the courthouse — 350 filled up the whole courthouse, you see. So our lawyer called for a mistrial because the public couldn't get in."

Red chuckled as he remembered back. "They let 'em all go but the ten leaders. I was one of the ten. We came up for trial the next day. The stool-pigeon who was in the pogey with us was up givin' evidence in the witness box."

"The stool-pigeon? Who was he?" Billy wanted to know.

"The police always planted a stoolie wherever there was a bunch of unemployed together. They wanted to know what was goin' on," Red grinned.

"Was the stoolie a kind of spy?"

"Yeah, that's what you'd call him," agreed Red. "A yellow-livered spy. Anyway, this guy's up givin' evidence about everybody, but he misses me. So the lawyer points this out to the judge, and the judge lets me go. They kept the others. Some of 'em got six months. Some got two years."

Red shook his head. "That pogey never opened again after that. A short time later they started shippin' us out to the relief camps."

Red's story and everything Billy was experiencing convinced him more and more that the Trek was really important. Prime Minister Bennett was the highest official in the land. When he realized how many Canadians were affected by not having jobs, he would get the government to do something to help them. He'd *have* to do something, Billy was sure of it.

Sometimes on top of the train, Billy would sit, his body bumping gently up and down with the movement of the carriage, and think about the prime minister. He wasn't quite sure what Mr. Bennett would look like, but he imagined himself meeting him and shaking hands with him.

Perhaps the prime minister would even say something like, "And what's a young man like you doing out of school, Billy?" And then Billy would explain about his dad losing his job and the family not having enough food to eat.

Billy put all kinds of twists to the story. Sometimes he imagined the prime minister taking him to lunch. He'd heard that Mr. Bennett always lived in a first-class hotel. Billy had never eaten in a hotel himself, but he supposed a person ate really well there.

He spent hours thinking about the fantastic meal he and Mr. Bennett would eat together. Dish after dish of all his favourite food — hot chicken soup with lots of noodles floating in it, steaming roast beef swimming in gravy, and baked potatoes slathered in creamy butter. For dessert he could never decide if they'd have strawberry shortcake or thick apple pie, so hot it melted the ice cream sitting on top of it....

Then Billy would smile to himself. After a while it seemed the train wheels, rattling along the steel tracks, began to sing: "*On to Ottawa, on to Ottawa, on to Ottawa.*"

12

A Change of Plans

AS the trekkers' freight pulled out of Moose Jaw, it headed into a fierce storm. There was no shelter from the driving rain up on top of the boxcars. The trekkers just put their heads down and hunched up their shoulders.

By the time the first pale patches of dawn crept over the land, the rain had stopped. The men riding the freight were left shivering. They huddled closer together, trying to keep warm while their clothes dried out in the cool early-morning air.

Steve couldn't stop sneezing, but it didn't make him one bit less excited as the train drew closer and closer to Regina. He could hardly sit still. This flat, brown land was his country. The prairies! A land where it seemed you could see clear across Saskatchewan and back into Alberta.

Dotted between the wide flat stretches were solid red barns and neat white farmhouses. Sometimes they'd pass a sad-looking group of white-faced cattle standing bored around a muddy hole. Once, as the train clattered by a bunch of tall reeds, it startled some wild geese. They took off at once, flying in perfect formation, one wing dipped low, their necks stretched out ahead of them.

To Billy, who had grown up with the mountains and the sea, these never-ending plains were a whole new world. Steve was about the best guide he could have had. He told Billy about gophers and sloughs and cottonwood bluffs.

"This storm we've had is really a blessing," he said, pulling his wet jacket up a bit higher around his neck and sneezing again.

Billy laughed. "It hasn't done you one bit of good," he told him.

"You're right there, but my dad will be pleased about it. We've hardly had any rain at all in the past two or three years. Normally, there are sloughs dotted all over like little lakes."

Steve pointed out a few deep depressions in the fields, all covered over with short grassy stubble. They looked like big dry pot-holes. Billy found it hard to believe the sloughs could be marshy swamps filled with water.

"One storm won't change the drought much. But it will help," Steve added. And he gave another terrific sneeze. "When I was a kid, we used to go down to a slough in the spring and catch birds," he went on. "One year I caught a pelican that hurt its wing. I took it home until its wing got better. We had no fish, so I had to catch frogs to feed it. You wouldn't think a pelican would be much of a pet, but it got to be real friendly. I called it Snow White because of its colour. Then in the fall my dad said I should let it go because it was too big to keep in captivity. It's wingspan by the end of the summer was over eight feet. It was hard to let it go. I half expected the next spring it might come back, but I never saw it again."

Even though years had passed since then, Steve's voice sounded sad as he talked about the pelican. Billy found himself looking over the plain, trying to see a big white bird, eight feet across, flying toward them. Other than a few crows, there wasn't much to be seen in the sky as the train hurried along.

"Do you keep a lot of animals on the farm?" Billy asked Steve.

"Not any more," Steve answered. "When I left we were down to two horses. We didn't have feed for any more. And we had to eat all the pigs. We've got a few chickens, of course, and two or three cows. Then my brother Tommy has got his prairie dog Whiskey, and we've got a real dog, who we call Grandad."

"That's a pretty funny name for a dog," Billy commented.

"My mum says he always looked like a tired old man even when he was a puppy, so we started calling him Grandad right from the beginning. Now he must be sixteen years old, and the name really suits him."

Billy was looking forward to meeting Steve's family and getting to know the farm. And Whiskey and Grandad, too!

Before long the train started to move through streets and warehouses. Gradually, it slowed down. At about six o'clock, it puffed to a stop in the railway yards.

There were crowds of people there waiting to welcome them. Billy stood up and stretched out. His whole body was stiff and aching and all his clothes were damp. Beside him, Steve was still sneezing nonstop.

"There he is!" a shrill voice called out. "Steve! Steve! Hey Steve, it's me!"

A small figure, blond and exactly like a smaller edition of Steve, darted out from the crowd. He ran among the idle locomotives and the empty boxcars until he stood right below them.

"It's my brother Tommy," Steve said with a grin all over his face.

Within seconds he was down on the ground. He picked up the small boy, put him on his shoulders and marched with everyone else along Tenth Avenue to the stadium in Regina.

Steve's father, marching along beside them, looked very proud and happy. He told Steve they'd left the farm while it was still dark in order to be in Regina to meet the freight.

"But we can't stay long," he explained. "Tommy's doing his exams today, so he should be back at school by nine."

Tommy groaned a bit at that and said it really wasn't important if he missed one old exam. His father wouldn't hear of it. The Trek was going to stop for two or three days in Regina before moving on, and Mr. Everchuk promised to be back before then to pick them up and take them out to the farm.

"Your mother and your sister and your other brothers can hardly wait to see you," he added with a big smile. "We'll have a real party out there, you'll see."

But nothing in Regina went according to plan, and it was several days before Billy and Steve got out to the farm.

When they first arrived in Regina, everything started off with promise. At the stadium, where they were billeted, there was a terrific breakfast waiting for them. While they ate, they were serenaded by the choir from the Ukrainian Farmer Labour Temple. The choir ended up with "Hold the Fort." Every single man in the place stood up and sang along with them. Steve had almost lost his voice by this time, but even he croaked along with the rest of them. At that minute it seemed nothing could go wrong.

As long as they were in Saskatchewan, the provincial government promised two meals a day for every trekker. In short order the men got busy organizing all the usual activities — a tag day to raise money and a big public meeting to tell the people what they were after.

But the newspapers were disturbing. They started to carry stories about the three hundred extra Mounties now in the Regina barracks and about the troop of soldiers that had been brought in from Sarcee Camp in Calgary.

Rumours were flying fast and loose. Everyone had a different story. Some said the government would stop the Trek here in Regina. Others said the men would be forced into a camp. Someone else was convinced they'd all be put in jail.

No one was put in jail or forced into a camp. Not yet. What did happen was that two cabinet ministers from Mr. Bennett's government arrived in Regina. They brought the trekkers an offer from the prime minister. He would meet with a small group of the trekkers and hear what they had to say.

The men discussed this long and hard. Most of them felt it would be better for them all to go to Ottawa just as they had planned. They were two thousand strong now, and another three thousand unemployed were waiting to join them in Winnipeg. Five thousand trekkers would make an impressive sight in front of the Parliament buildings in Ottawa. Steve favoured this plan, and Billy wanted them all to go to Ottawa, too. He'd dreamed so much about them being there in front of the Parliament buildings. He knew exactly what they looked like. His history book that year had a picture of Parliament Hill. Billy had studied it carefully before he left home so that he'd know what to expect. The elegant towers with their green copper roofs high on the hill in front of the river were an important part of his dreams about meeting the prime minister personally. Yet Billy was learning that you can't always do things exactly as you might like. Sometimes you have to compromise and give in a bit.

When Jack said reluctantly, "I don't see we have much option. All along we've said we want a chance to meet with Bennett to present our demands. We can hardly refuse his offer now to talk to us," Billy was inclined to agree with him. Perhaps the prime minister really wanted to hear what they had to say, and he might have something important to tell them, too.

Whenever the trekkers had something to decide, every single person could speak his mind if he wanted. It meant the discussions often went on and on for hours, but in the long run it seemed the best way to operate. When the trekkers finally did reach a decision about something, all the men were usually convinced it was the best thing to do.

That was the way they came to their decision about meeting the prime minister. After long debate, a vote was finally taken, and they settled on sending a delegation of eight to speak for them in Ottawa.

The eight trekkers set out on the morning of June

19, 1935. This time they didn't ride on top of a freight train. They travelled inside a first-class compartment — "on the cushions" as the men called it. Everyone was down at the station to see them off.

Once the passenger train pulled out, the men who were left behind in Regina had nothing much to do but wait. On that day, Pete Everchuk came in from the farm and picked up Billy and Steve to go out and visit the family.

13

Out to the Farm

BILLY always remembered everything about that day on the Everchuk farm. Pete Everchuk came to pick them up early in the morning. He was driving the family car, only not in the way that one would expect. It was an ordinary black Ford sedan all right, but the engine had been removed and the collapsible hood folded back. Except for the farm horse hitched up in front of it, the car looked much the way it was supposed to when it came out of Henry Ford's factory in Windsor, Ontario.

"Welcome to our Bennett buggy," Steve's father told him. "It's named after our prime minister, the Honourable R. B. Bennett." His voice sounded sarcastic. Billy guessed that Mr. Bennett was no more popular with the Prairie farmers than he was with the unemployed workers out in British Columbia.

"We've no money for gas to run a car," Mr. Everchuk explained as the two boys climbed in the back seat. "So we use horses! As long as we keep air in the tires, the old Bennett buggy is easier to pull than a farm wagon."

And that was how they drove to the farm outside Regina. Pete Everchuk, the golden whiskers on his face trailing in the wind, stood up behind the steering wheel, holding on to the reins. Billy and Steve sat in the back seat, talking ten to the dozen about the Trek and the reception they'd been getting from people across the country.

"And what do you feel about this meeting with Bennett?" Pete Everchuk asked in a serious voice.

"It's hard to know what he's up to this time," Steve told him.

"But now that he sees there's so many of us, he's going to have to help us," Billy added.

"Humph," Mr. Everchuk said in answer, and he gave the old mare a flick on the rump as she trotted along the road leading out to the country.

No sooner were they at the farm than Mrs. Everchuk began fussing over the boys. It seemed to Billy as if it had been a long time since he had left Vancouver and had anyone fussing over him. Although the farmhouse sitting there on the wide-open plain was a far cry from his own little wooden house on Cameroon Street, Billy felt very homesick.

Everyone wanted to do everything all at once. The Everchuks were a family of five children, and they all had different ideas about what Billy and Steve were to see first. Tommy wanted them to meet Whiskey; Niki wanted them to see his painting; Larissa wanted to show them her new foal; Mike wanted to talk about the Trek; and Mrs. Everchuk wanted to put a hot compress on Steve's chest to get rid of his cough. Fortunately, they had the whole day ahead of them. There would be time for everything.

First they met Whiskey. He was the striped gopher that Tommy had caught.

"I like to call him a prairie dog," Tommy said seriously. "It makes him sound more like a pet, don't you think?"

He told Billy how easy it had been to catch Whiskey. "All you do is this. When you find a gopher hole in the ground, you tie a noose in a piece of twine and place the noose part over the hole. Then you lie down to wait. You've got to be very quiet because gophers have very keen hearing. Down there in his hole the gopher probably knows there's something happening up above ground. A gopher is so curious that before long he'll come up to investigate. And you've got to be ready for him. You pull the twine tight enough to rope him in but not so tight you hurt him.

"It's a cinch to do," Tommy assured him. "Though this year there aren't too many gophers around. With the drought and all, there aren't even enough weeds for them to eat." And he rubbed his finger along the back of Whiskey's head and gave him a few crumbs from his pocket.

Whiskey nibbled them hungrily. Then he stood up on his hind legs, stretching his head high as if he were trying to see what was happening over on the next farm. He really was a curious fellow.

Larissa's new foal was called Trekkie. Billy had never seen a new-born foal before. He was amazed at the way it frisked around on its spindly legs. Sometimes its legs would give way and it would slide around looking pretty silly. It didn't want to go too far from its mother. She kept an eye on anyone who came near it. Every now and again she'd put her neck over the foal's back and nuzzle it gently.

Inside the barn there was a layer of threshed wheat straw over the floor for the three cows to bed down on. Billy laughed when he saw it.

"Hey Steve, this is how we're sleeping, too."

And it was. At the stadium in Regina the floor had been covered with straw, and on that the two thousand trekkers had to sleep. The stadium didn't have the kind of artwork gracing its walls that the Everchuks' cows had. On the big back wall of the barn Niki had painted a huge map of Canada. The coast lines were drawn carefully in blue with PACIFIC OCEAN and ATLANTIC OCEAN printed carefully along each side. Black lines separated each province, and in each space Niki had painted BC, ALTA, SASK, MAN, ONT, QUE, NB, PEI, NS.

It was a pretty fair map except that Niki had got a bit mixed up around Hudson Bay. It ended up almost touching the Great Lakes, though you could easily tell what it was supposed to be.

Out of a newspaper he'd cut a picture of the trekkers getting up on top of the boxcars. This picture was now stuck right where Regina was marked. Stretching behind it in a red dotted line was the train track all the way from Vancouver.

"Every day I come out and add a bit to it," Niki told them. "I've got loads of red paint to get you to Ottawa," he said proudly.

Ottawa was on the map, but Niki had had to squeeze it in a bit between James Bay and Lake Ontario, not too far from the Quebec border. He had marked it with a huge X.

"In school we talk about the Trek all the time. Our teacher's got a big map on the blackboard, and we keep moving the train along there, too," Niki said. "I think she's got a personal interest in the Trek," he continued with a grin. "She wants to get married, but her boyfriend can't get a job anywhere. He's going to join up if the Trek gets going again."

Everything about the day seemed wonderful to Billy—the farm, the family, the dinner they ate together. Mrs. Everchuk cooked up the biggest pot of beans Billy had ever seen, with bits of sausage floating in it. Although it looked as if there'd be enough for two or three meals, the brown earthenware casserole was empty by the time they were through.

"Even with the drought we haven't suffered too much," Steve's mother said as she put two more heaping plates of beans in front of the boys. "Farmers from Ontario have sent us carloads of vegetables, and from B.C. we've got barrels of Macintosh apples."

"As long as we all stick together, I guess we'll get by," Mr. Everchuk added, stroking his beard.

That night, before Pete Everchuk drove them back to Regina, Larissa handed Billy a pretty wooden doll, her dress painted in red and yellow. The doll could be separated in two, and inside was a little sister painted in exactly the same way. Inside her was another, and then another, and another, and another. In the end there were six little Russian girls standing side by side. They all wore blue kerchiefs over their heads, and each one was a little smaller than the one before.

"Keep this as a present for your sister," Larissa told Billy shyly. "I've had it for a long time and I'd like her to have it now. I hope it will remind you and Helen of us." She gave him a quick kiss on his cheek, and Billy's face turned as red as his hair.

It was very late when Billy and Steve got back to the stadium. As Billy tried to get comfortable in his straw bed, he held the wooden doll and rubbed his fingers over the smooth head. Larissa's head had been smooth, too, her long blond hair reaching almost to her waist.

Maybe, he thought, she and Steve and Tommy and Niki and Mike and their parents would all come out to Vancouver for a holiday. If the Higginses could ever afford a car again, the two families could go over to Vancouver Island on the ferry. They'd go fishing and swimming, and they'd hunt for pieces of jade on the beach. He knew his father would like Mr. Everchuk.

They'd have a great time together. But first they'd have to do something about the Depression, he decided. Right now no one could even think of taking holidays anywhere.

Perhaps the prime minister would help them. That was the last thought Billy had before he fell fast asleep.

14

The Prime Minister's Answer

BILLY was angry. Every time he took a step he kicked the toe of his right boot against the ground. It was as if he were kicking the devil out of someone.

The two boys walked along side by side in the lines of men marching back to the stadium for breakfast. It was not quite eight o'clock in the morning, but already the late June sun was high in the blue sky.

They had woken up early that morning to be down at the railway station by seven. That was when the train bringing the delegation back from Ottawa was due in at Regina.

There were too many trekkers to all fit into the big grey train station, so most of them waited outside in the parking lot. Jammed in the crowd, Billy could hardly see the eight men as they came out of the station and into the sunshine, but he cheered and clapped along with the others. Then Slim Evans climbed on the bumper of a taxi so that the trekkers could get a better look at him as he explained what had happened in Ottawa. You could have heard a pin drop out there on the parking lot in front of the high, vaulted railway station. Billy kept his eyes rivetted on Slim's tired-looking face as he told them the news.

Prime Minister Bennett had refused to help them. What's more, he wouldn't let them go one mile further east on the freights. A relief camp was waiting for them outside of Regina. All relief in the city itself was to be cut off after breakfast.

Billy could hardly believe his ears.

"It's a bad situation," Evans told them. "But we've got a couple of cards up our sleeves yet."

"I knew all the time the government wouldn't help us," Steve muttered now between tight lips. "They never intended to do anything," he went on.

Billy didn't answer him. He felt confused. He'd always believed that the prime minister would find some solution to their problems. There were now well over two thousand trekkers in Regina, and every day men from other parts of Saskatchewan kept coming into the city to join them. Maybe Mr. Bennett didn't realize just how many of them were involved. Maybe he thought they wanted fancy jobs with big salaries. Maybe he didn't realize they just wanted work and wages so they'd feel useful again and have enough to eat and not have to quit school just to get relief and... Maybe. Maybe. Maybe.

Everything swam around in Billy's head all jumbled together. He wished he could talk to Slim Evans himself. He wanted to be sure they'd told Mr. Bennett exactly what the situation was. But Slim and the others were somewhere out in front of the long column of men marching back to the stadium. Billy wished he could at least see Jack and find out what he thought about it all.

All during breakfast Billy searched and searched for Jack's shiny bald head. His eyes went up and down the lengths of wooden planks that were set up as dining tables in the stadium. There was no sign of Jack McGooley.

Billy didn't say a word to anyone as he ate the overcooked oatmeal porridge from the tin plate. Questions raced around in his head, looking for answers. How would they continue to eat if relief were cut off? Who'd feed them? For two whole months in Vancouver they'd taken up collections to feed the striking camp workers. Now, after nearly a whole month travelling, they couldn't just start all over again. And they were so far from home! The little wooden house on Cameroon Street seemed like a world away now.

"I'm getting out of here and going for a walk, Bill. Want to come?" Steve asked him.

Billy shook his head. "I haven't finished yet," he mumbled without looking up.

Steve shrugged and walked away.

Most of the men had by now wandered out of the

building. A few still lingered on with their cigarettes and the dregs of coffee in their mugs. Billy sat by himself, the last few spoonfuls of messy oatmeal in the bottom of the tin plate.

At one end of the long hall a small group of men stood around in a circle. Every now and again they'd break out in wild laughter. Then Billy heard Jack's distinctive guffaws. It wasn't that Jack laughed louder than anyone else. It was just that while most people laugh as they let their breath out, Jack made his guffaws while he took in deep mouthfuls of air.

The boy got up and went toward the circle, thinking Jack might have a poker game going there. As he drew closer, he could hear a voice from somewhere in the middle of the group.

"We arrived in Ottawa around three in the morning. Got off the train and an RCMP policeman was there to meet us. He took us to the hotel where we were goin' to stay. It was a hotel that had been closed and they opened it up for us. There was nobody stayin' there but us. At eleven-thirty the next morning we were supposed to meet the government for one half hour. Well, we were in there an hour and a half. We met Mr. Prime Minister Bennett and his cabinet. There were ten or eleven of them."

Billy recognized the voice of Red Walsh.

"Where did you meet with the brass, Red?" someone asked.

"We met in one of the cabinet offices," Walsh answered. "A red carpet on the floor. A big long table it was and Bennett was sittin' right in the centre. Bennett had on a swallowtail coat and the collar with the wings and a dotted tie. He was so stiff and starchy, he'd squeak when he moved. I had on overalls. So did Evans. He had a pair of those combination overalls, and under that was his underwear. That was all he wore.

"We looked like eight tramps in there. Bennett was sittin' across the table, and first he found out that none of us was born in the country, only Evans. Then he said, 'You have been in jail in Westminster Penitentiary, Mr. Evans?'

"'No,' said Evans. 'I have never been in jail in Westminster Penitentiary.'

"'You were arrested in Drumheller, Alberta. You were charged with theft and you did time.'

"Evans got up, walked over and put his hands on the table and looked at him, eyeball to eyeball. 'You're a liar, Mr. Bennett,' he said to him. 'I was never in jail in Westminster Penitentiary and I was never arrested for theft. You're a lawyer, Mr. Bennett. You should know that. You're lyin' to the people as you did in 19 and 30 when you were elected.'"

There were loud hoots from all the men in the group, and Jack let out another series of his guffaws too. The men were obviously pleased that Slim had told Mr. Bennett he was a liar. Billy knew they'd have loved to have said the same to him if they could.

He'd heard his father talk a lot about Mr. Bennett.

The man had made a lot of promises when he was running for election in 1930. He had said he'd get the country on its feet again and put everybody back to work. He was going to make things good for Canadians. So they had elected his Conservative government and put them in power. Prime Minister Bennett had not kept his promises, and this was something no one was prepared to excuse. They felt tricked and angry.

When the laughter had died down a bit, Red continued with his story. "Bennett himself was very hostile," he went on. "Only two or three of the other government people spoke, and, of course, they spoke against us. The Mounties were all around, and the newspaper reporters were up on the transoms of the doors, tryin' to get everything they could.

"Then Bennett told us, 'We'll send the necessary forces north, south, east and west to stop trouble-makers like you.'"

"He'll try it, too," said Jack. "And the yellow-legged hummingbirds will do his dirty work for him."

Yellow-legged hummingbirds was the way the trekkers referred to the RCMP, now gathering in huge numbers around Regina. It was a neat name, Billy thought. The yellow stripes on their uniforms made them look long-legged and spindly, just like birds. There wasn't much love lost between the unemployed trekkers and the Mounties, who were being sent to police them and keep them off any freights going east.

The group of men began to break up. Red Walsh hurried off, muttering that there was no time to stand around any longer. He had work to do.

"So, Billy, what d'ya think of the turn of events?" Jack asked him, putting his arm around the boy's narrow shoulders.

"I don't know much what to think, Jack. I can't believe the prime minister refused to help us. What's going to happen to us now?" Billy got the words out quickly, nervously biting the nail on his little finger.

Jack didn't even smile. "That's a good question, Billy. But we won't answer it yakking here all day. Let's go down to the strike office and see if they need help."

15

Down to the Last Forty Cents

THE strike office was set up in the Unemployed Hall in downtown Regina. When Billy and Jack got there, the place was in an uproar. No sooner had they walked in the door than someone told Jack to go down to city hall with two other men to meet with Regina's Mayor Rink. Slim Evans and two or three others were already on their way to the Parliament buildings to see Mr. Gardiner, the premier of Saskatchewan. The trekkers needed help from somewhere.

"Give the kid something useful to do," Jack said to Red Walsh before he left.

Red put Billy to work minding the phone.

"Calls will be comin' in with offers of trucks to get us out of the city," he explained. "Word's got out they won't let us back on top of the freights, so we're gonna try to make it to Ottawa by truck."

Billy was pleased they weren't going to give up—that the Trek was on again. He was still sure that when the prime minister saw them all together he'd realize how important it was that something be done to help them. Surely so many people couldn't be ignored by the leader of the country.

Red told Billy what he had to do. "Take the name, address, telephone number, and the size of the truck. Ask whoever you're talking to how many guys their truck will hold and whether or not it'll come with a driver."

The phone hardly stopped ringing. By the end of an hour and a half Billy had two whole pages filled with names, addresses, and enough trucks to carry seven hundred men.

Normally, Billy wasn't a very neat writer. One of his teachers, Miss Petersen, had always grumbled that his compositions looked like a hen had walked across the page. Now he made sure that the names and numbers he wrote down were very clear. He knew it was important that the trekkers be able to get in touch with these people again.

When Billy told Steve about the trucks being offered to get them further east, Steve wondered if his father might be able to lend the old Bennett buggy. They decided that it wouldn't be very practical. The old farm mare could take forever to get as far as Ottawa.

For the next two days Billy continued to work in the strike office. He didn't get back on the phone again and was disappointed about that, but there was a lot of other work to be done. Then, abruptly, the whole truck idea had to be dropped.

Billy was in the office on Friday afternoon, running off leaflets on the stencil machine. The leaflets said that the trekkers refused to be forced into the Lumsden Relief Camp. Suddenly, one of the men came out of a small office to say he'd just had a phone call from Ottawa. Mr. Bennett's cabinet had passed a special law, an order-in-council, that gave the police in Regina extraordinary powers.

The men in the strike office didn't have to wait long to learn what this meant. Within an hour the RCMP chief in Regina, Assistant-Commissioner Wood, told them that he had orders to stop all movement. The camp strikers would not be allowed further east whether it was by rail, truck, car, bus or foot. And that wasn't all. Any person caught assisting the strikers in any way — giving them food, shelter or transportation — would be prosecuted.

"This really changes everything for us," grumbled Jack McGooley as he stroked down the wispy grey hairs just above his neck.

Billy didn't quite understand what Jack meant — at least, he didn't understand until the phone calls started coming in about the truck offers. It seemed that most of the people who had volunteered their trucks now thought that the trucks might not be free for the trekkers to use after all.

"They're just scared, Billy, and you can hardly

blame them," Jack told him. "We're being painted as the bad guys in this story. But those yellow-legged hummingbirds ain't got us yet."

Later that afternoon Billy heard Red Walsh telling Jack that there was less than $1,200 left in the trekkers' kitty. Each man would be given forty cents and that would have to do him for two meals. That was all there was. There'd be nothing left after that.

Billy knew he'd be able to stretch his forty cents into three meals. He still had five cents left of the two dollars that his father had given him nearly a month ago. And he'd found a greasy-spoon café where they offered a trekkers' special of peas, meat pie and potatoes for only fifteen cents.

Right now though, Billy wasn't thinking of himself. He was thinking that in one more day there'd be no more money to feed the two thousand trekkers now in Regina. Worse yet, anyone caught giving them help of any kind would be arrested. Some people were already in jail. The Relief Camp Workers' Union had been declared an illegal organization.

All that weekend, even on Sunday, Slim Evans and the other strike leaders were meeting with Premier Gardiner and representatives of the Ottawa government. It hadn't taken the trekkers long to decide they'd have to give up the Trek. They'd asked to be allowed to return to their homes and were more than prepared to travel on top of the freight trains to do so.

Some of the trekkers were going into the city to the meeting at Market Square where Slim Evans was going to speak. The meeting would tell the people what the trekkers had decided. Most of the trekkers, though, were planning to be at the big baseball game at the exhibition grounds.

"Come to the game, Billy," Steve urged. "There's nothing else to do around here. And you've never seen Casey Donovan bat. That guy could hit a homer on a pinhead coming from Ottawa, I swear it."

Steve was crazy about baseball. He was always talking about Casey Donovan, one of the trekkers from White Rock, who hit home runs every game he played.

That Sunday was July 1. Dominion Day. Canada's sixty-eighth birthday. Billy didn't feel there was very much to celebrate. Anyway, Jack had already asked Billy if he'd go down to the Unemployed Hall with him and Red Walsh. They were going to work on a press release, so Billy passed up the game at the exhibition grounds, preferring to go into town with Jack and Red.

16

The Riot in Market Square

NO sooner had the Strike Committee begun to work on the press release, than the door burst open. One of the trekkers stood there, his clothes dirty and his face flushed.

He was so excited and talked so quickly that no one could understand what he was trying to say. Then gradually, it came out that the Market Square meeting had been broken up by policemen who had arrived in three furniture vans. They had forced their way into the square, throwing tear-gas bombs and firing their rifles. Already one person had been killed.

Horrified, Billy looked to Jack for some explanation. Jack was muttering under his breath, "The sons of...," on and on, over and over. Billy didn't need any further explanation.

The Unemployed Hall was only three short blocks from where the meeting was held. Billy, Jack and the others ran over to the big, open square behind the market, which by now was in shambles. Men, women and children were running in all directions. Policemen, threatening the crowd with clubs and bats, were running after them. Shots were being fired, and over on one side of the square there seemed to be a lot of smoke.

By now, Red Walsh had climbed up on a garbage can and was trying to get the trekkers to march back to the stadium. A shot whizzed past his ear and into the concrete wall behind him. He dropped down into the garbage can.

"Good God!" Billy heard him say. "The cops sure aren't kiddin' around!"

Everything happened very quickly after that. Billy hardly knew what he was doing. People were running everywhere, yelling and looking for cover. Jack grabbed Billy's shirt and pulled him over to where some of the men had lined up.

"Keep your cool, men. March straight back to the stadium and stay there," yelled Red.

They'd only gone two blocks when two hundred Mounted Police appeared in the street just ahead of them. In an attempt to defend themselves, the marching trekkers pushed the parked cars lining the streets onto their sides, piling them one on top of the other, two cars high.

The Mounties were getting closer all the time. Desperately the men behind the piled cars started to pick up bricks and stones from the roadway. They threw them wildly at the horses marching toward them. As they let the first rocks fly, the front line of horses started to panic and bolted down a side street. Still the rows of Mounties kept coming in straight, tense lines. The men behind the overturned cars kept up their barrage of stones, but before long they'd used up everything that they could lay their hands on.

Then from behind the barricade, boys and girls on bicycles started pedalling up, their carrier baskets loaded with rocks. They dumped them behind the barricade and then rode off quickly to get another load.

When Billy saw the rocks piling up behind the stacked cars, he felt they weren't alone anymore. Some of the children were no older than Helen. Helen! This gave him a terrific idea.

In his pocket Billy always carried the slingshot she'd made for his birthday. He hadn't used it since picking off that old man's hat back in Vancouver, except for target practice at fenceposts during the long trip from the West Coast. Now he took it out and pulled taut the strong, tan rubber sling. It was in good working order. For a brief moment he thought of the time he had shot stones at the side of Old Tomlin's shed. He had been just a kid then, playing around with a kid's toy. It hadn't been so long ago, but right now it seemed like a million years. He felt so much older, and these days there was no time for fooling around. His slingshot might help him get out of a very serious situation.

Quickly he picked up a nice, sharp stone, shaped like

a tiny grey triangle, with little sparkles in the cutting edge. He slotted the stone in the rubber cradle of the slingshot, pulled back the sling, took careful aim, and bingo! A bull's-eye right in the fat, glossy black rump of one of the policemen's horses. The horse edged away, stumbling in the crowd. Billy felt a twinge of pity for the poor beast. Still, the horse would get over it, and this fight was more important. He scooped up another rock and made another bull's-eye. This time the horse, a nervous roan, bucked and whinnied, throwing its policeman rider to the pavement.

"Hey kid, you been prepared for trouble all along," Jack grinned at him as he stood up and let fly another rock himself. Right after he said that, Jack doubled over and fell to the ground beside Billy with a dull thud.

"Jack, you alright?" Billy asked him, half thinking Jack was just acting up and pretending he'd been hit. Then he saw that out of Jack's chest a flood of thick red blood was spurting.

"God help us," said one of the men on the other side of the slumped body. "They've hit McGooley."

For a minute Billy couldn't move. He watched as the other man took off his shirt and held it over the wound in Jack's chest.

"Don't just stand there, kid, or you'll get it too. Get down and hold this over his chest. Take your shirt off, too. We'll need all the rags we can find."

Billy didn't know how long he crouched down there beside Jack, watching him trying to speak and seeing all that blood. By the time two men came in from behind the barricade with a stretcher and lifted Jack onto it, Billy was sure there couldn't be any blood left in the big man's body. Where he'd been lying, there was a large red stain on the ground.

Billy didn't want to leave his friend, but one of the men with the red-cross armbands said they'd take good care of him. He told Billy to stay with the other trekkers and go back to the stadium.

"Just wanted to prove it to you, kid. I'm a real red-blooded type," Jack whispered with a kind of twisted smile. Then they took him off.

In a daze Billy and the other men marched back to the stadium. The police had finally disappeared. There was hardly a soul to be seen. Broken glass and bricks and rocks littered the streets; street lamps and store windows were shattered. It looked like a city at war, Billy thought. But that was impossible, he kept telling himself angrily. This was Saskatchewan, Canada. Wars don't happen here!

"We just want work and wages," he said to himself. It was no reason to shoot at Jack. Marching along with the men, Billy became aware of the hot, salty tears running down his cheeks. He almost never cried and certainly never in public. Now he didn't care. He knew these were not the tears of a crybaby, but tears of anger. Anger at the police who had shot his friend Jack, and anger at Mr. Bennett, who didn't care what happened to people like Billy and his friends.

It was very dark when Billy reached the stadium and fell onto his straw bed. He slept through a night of dreams. Each more frightening than the last.

In the morning the situation was worse than ever. Barbed wire had been strung up around the stadium. Billy could count at least six machine guns mounted on the roofs of the buildings around the grounds. Mounties stood guard behind the guns, the black muzzles aimed down on the stadium.

Billy went back to his straw bed and lay down. Steve tried to talk to him, but Billy wouldn't roll over or even open his eyes. He stayed like that all morning until Red Walsh came in to see him.

"It's no use tryin' to hide from it all, Billy. You gotta face the facts and deal with them best you can."

Red told Billy that Slim Evans and at least a hundred of the other trekkers were in jail. "I just been at the hospital with Jack. He asked me to tell you he's fine. They're pumpin' new blood into him so fast he'll probably be out before you know it."

Billy was relieved, but he still said nothing. The anger inside him was changing to another kind of feeling. Billy knew he would never forget what he had seen the day before. He knew that he was going to spend all his energies from now on trying to make sure that men like Jack would never again be treated so unjustly, to make sure that bloodshed of the kind he had seen that day would never happen again. He did not know quite how he was going to accomplish this, but he would. Suddenly, Billy felt calmer. He would *do* something. *He*, Billy Higgins. As his mother had often said, nobody would ever dare mess with Billy Higgins when he had set his mind on a thing.

Jack McGooley was not out of hospital the following Friday when the trekkers finally took a train back to their homes. This time, by agreement with the government of Mr. Bennett, they went "on the cushions." They even had sandwiches and coffee supplied for them.

Steve didn't go back on the train to the West Coast either, but instead returned to his family's farm outside Regina. He and the whole Everchuk family were there to see Billy and the others off at the station.

"Don't worry about your friend Jack," Mrs. Everchuk told Billy. "When they let him out of hospital, we'll take him to the farm until he's well enough to go back to Vancouver."

Billy felt a bit as if he were leaving his own family when the train pulled out.

"Take care of yourself, Billy," Steve called out. "I'm going to come out and see you all again, soon as I get a bit of money together. You can be sure of that."

As the train moved off and passed through the peaceful-looking farmlands on the outskirts of Regina, Billy wondered when he would see them again. It was hard to be sure of anything anymore. He knew that now.

17

Home Again

DESPITE the defeat, the train ride back to the West Coast was a lively affair. Even Billy felt excited and strong, although he couldn't figure out why. Maybe it was just the fact of riding inside, in a warm, comfortable carriage, instead of outside on top in the wind and rain.

Jack had asked Red Walsh to keep an eye on his young friend until they got to Vancouver, so Red kept Billy close by him.

"We haven't lost the battle, Billy," Red said. "We just haven't got the strength to go on right now. But we still got our organization. If the situation doesn't change, we'll pull the camps out again."

When the passenger train chugged to a full stop at the Vancouver station, Sam Higgins was there. He was standing all by himself, his hands in his pockets, waiting for Billy.

He looked tired, and a lot older. Billy was surprised

to find that his dad seemed smaller, somehow. Then he realized that really he had not changed all that much. But, he, Billy Higgins, wasn't the boy he'd been when he'd last seen his father; he was becoming a man.

"You've grown, son," said his father, nodding his head in approval. "And you look all tanned and healthy, too. I guess the trip was good for you."

They stood in shy silence for a moment. Then suddenly, Sam put his arms around his son and hugged him tight. "I'd better get you home to your mother. She's been worried sick about you," he said.

"You're lucky you weren't killed," said his mother. "I knew Helen should never have given you that slingshot. It was just asking for trouble."

Billy grinned at her. By now he understood that his mother's style of talking was just a bluff to hide the way she really felt.

"Come on, Mum," he teased. "Aren't you the least bit proud of me?"

"Oh sure. Proud as punch to have you out there in Dutch with the law, and shooting rocks at the police. What more could a mother ask?"

But she smiled at him in spite of herself, for she knew that the police action in Regina had been a disgrace and that her son had acted bravely.

"I suppose you'll be out robbing stores, now that you're back home," she said, but she was kidding with him. "When can we visit you next in jail?"

"No, Mum, I've got my future pretty well planned out. First, I've got to get back to school somehow. And then, I'm going to do something to get some of these problems straightened out."

"Oh Lord! What do you think you're going to be? A politician?" she said sharply. "That's all we need."

Billy hardly stopped talking all that night. There was so much to say. So many stories to tell. And Mary and Sam and Helen wanted to hear them all.

Out of his knapsack Billy took Larissa's pretty Russian doll and gave it to Helen. She unscrewed the painted wooden figure and took out the smaller dolls inside. The six little dolls with the saucy faces and the gaily painted skirts and kerchiefs were lined up in a row on the kitchen table.

"They're beautiful!" said Helen, her dark eyes glowing.

"One day the whole Everchuk family is going to come out here for a holiday, and then you'll be able to thank Larissa yourself," Billy told her.

"I don't have to wait until then," Helen said. "I can write to her and tell her how much I like them."

It wasn't until the middle of October that Jack McGooley was strong enough to go back to Vancouver. When he did return, Billy and his father met him at the station and brought him home to dinner.

Jack looked much the same, though Billy noticed

that the wispy hair above his neck and the bushy brows over the piercing blue eyes were pure white now.

The very day Jack arrived was election day, October 14, 1935. Jack said he'd been able to vote before he left Regina. Sam and Mary had cast their ballots first thing that morning. Billy, of course, was still too young, though he knew exactly how he'd have voted.

At dinner time when Sam turned the radio on to the seven o'clock news, they heard that Canada had a new prime minister. R. B. Bennett had been defeated. Mackenzie King was going to form a new government.

"Billy m'boy, we've done it!" Jack shouted.

The CBC announcer reported that the people of Canada had withdrawn their support from the Bennett government after the Regina riot. "The On-to-Ottawa Trek showed Mr. Bennett that the government has to be more responsive to the country's workers," the voice on the radio went on.

"Hey, we *did* do it, after all!" Billy said, amazed. He had been thinking about the Trek a lot, wondering if their effort and hardship had meant anything after all. He was even beginning to ask himself if they had just made big fools of themselves, blundering across Canada only to be forced to give up in Regina. Now he saw that it hadn't been a defeat after all. They had acted, and their action had made a difference.

No one sitting around the kitchen table at 24 Cameroon Street heard another word of the broadcast. They all started talking at once as they congratulated each other. Jack said old Dickie Bennett had bitten off more than he could chew when he took on the unemployed workers in Canada.

Jack McGooley never went back to the relief camps. Through a friend he got a job in a paper mill in Ocean Falls. They offered him a dollar an hour, and Jack gladly took the job.

Billy never was sent to a relief camp. The camps were reorganized by the B.C. Forestry Department, and the camp workers started building parks and campgrounds around the province. They earned forty cents an hour. But by then Billy was working as a delivery boy for one of the local newspapers.

Sam couldn't find a job for more than a year. Finally, he was taken on at a small factory that made radio parts. While his wage wasn't anything near what it had been when he'd worked at Robertson's, with what he and Billy earned together it was enough for Billy to start back to school by taking night courses.

Billy and Sam worked it out that by studying through the summers, Billy would be able to finish high school in four years. Then he could enroll in an engineering course, or a history course, or anything else he wanted. Maybe he would even go and work on the Everchuk's farm with Steve. He had time to make up his mind — and even to change it.

The important thing now was that he had something to look forward to again. This made all the difference in the world.

THE END

Afterword

The story of Billy Higgins is fiction, but it is based on real events and the experiences of real people. The Trek was an actual event, as was the Regina riot. Police arrested 130 people after the riot and charged them with "disturbing the peace." Nine persons were given prison sentences. The rest were found not guilty or had charges against them dismissed.

Slim Evans and five other Trek leaders were charged with membership in an illegal organization — the Relief Camp Workers' Union. The charges against them were dropped for lack of evidence.

Red Walsh, Slim Evans and the government officials named were the only real people in the story. However, Canada in 1935 was full of courageous, adventurous, unemployed workers like Billy Higgins, Steve Everchuk and Jack McGooley. They all wanted to build decent lives for themselves and make the country a better place for everyone.